SECRETS
of the
BOOK

by ERIN FRY

two lions

twɔ lioɳs

Text copyright © 2014 Erin Fry
All rights reserved.

Published by Two Lions, New York

www.apub.com

ISBN-13: 9781477847169
ISBN-10: 1477847162

Book design by Ryan Michaels.

Library of Congress Cataloging-in-Publication Data
available upon request.

Printed in the United States of America
FIRST EDITION

To all the students of Rooms 208 and 109
who have and continue to teach me so much;
and to the many Gregors out there who prove
that having autism doesn't mean you can't save the world

Contents

CHAPTER 1
WHERE I MEET BABE RUTH
AND TRY NOT TO FREAK OUT

Sure, my eyesight has never been the greatest. And yeah, it was now rapidly on its way from "can't see jack" to "really can't see jack." But even my eye doctor, Dr. Burt, would tell you I wasn't blind. Yet. So there was a pretty good chance that I was actually seeing the three people in front of me. Which was impossible. Because they were dead.

With a not-so-quiet *whoosh*, I let out the breath I'd been holding. Then I closed my eyes and counted to three slowly.

Hesitantly, I opened my left eye and then my right. Then pushed my glasses up my nose.

And tried not to freak out.

All three of them were still there—moving,

smiling, *breathing*. How was this possible? I looked at Ed, whose grin stretched from one oversized, freckle-spotted ear to the other.

"Told ya, kid. It's the real deal," he said. Then he patted the large book that lay open across his lap and winked at me.

That's when I knew my legs were not going to hold me up. I fell back into the threadbare armchair behind me—a chair that I was positive was almost as old as Ed—and watched little dust motes swirl off into the air. I sneezed.

Babe Ruth looked up.

As if it were the most normal thing in the world, he said, "*Gesundheit*, kid." Then he continued to rub the wooden bat in his hands like I'd seen guys in the big leagues do right before they stepped up to the plate.

With shaky hands, I took off the heavy black-rimmed glasses that I have worn for most of my twelve years of life. Predictably, the world dissolved into a mess of blurry colors and hazy shapes. I wiped each thick lens on the hem of my T-shirt and placed them back in front of my eyes.

Nope, I wasn't imagining things. Babe Ruth—*the* Babe Ruth—was still standing there, having just blessed my sneeze.

"Ha! You didn't believe me, did you, Spencer?" Ed's eyes sparkled like a kid's on Christmas morning.

I couldn't speak. Babe Ruth—the Great Bambino—was standing, like, spitting distance from me. Next to him was an older guy in a wrinkled, gray V-neck sweater with a bushy mustache and a big— no, gigantic—nose. He was frantically scribbling a long list of figures and exponents on a small notepad. His bushy hair was almost completely white, and even if I'd had a comb to give him, there was no way it would have made it through that mess. I'd only seen one or two pictures of him, but this guy had to be Albert Einstein.

And across the room from me, fluffing out her perfect curls in the mirror over Ed's sink, was Marilyn Monroe. Ed had quickly explained that she was this actress from the 1950s who I guess had died sorta tragically. The way Ed was looking at her—like my old beagle used to look at a steak—she must have been smokin' hot back when she was alive. Jeez, she was smokin' right now!

Which, of course, was impossible.

Again, I may not have the best vision in the world, and though no one in my family likes to admit it, it's getting worse by the hour. But unless I was completely losing it, those three people were all very much alive and kicking. When they should have been very much dead. And still on the pages of that giant book Ed had.

Let me stop here for a second and back up. My mom always gets tweaked at me because I have this habit of jumping into the middle of the story. But really—isn't that where all the action is? Why waste your time on the whos and wheres and whats when you can get right to the good stuff? But my mom will no doubt read this at some point, and she loves whos and wheres and whats. So here goes. . . .

My name is Spencer Lemon—pronounced le-MONE, like you would if you were in France. *Not* like the sour yellow fruit. I'm just finishing up sixth grade at Lilac Junior High, which by the way has no lilac bushes growing anywhere near it that I know of. It does have a couple of palm trees, though. I guess Palm Tree Junior High didn't sound as good or something.

Every Tuesday and Thursday afternoon, my mom makes me hang out with Ed, an old guy who kicks it at the Everlasting Home for Seniors (a.k.a. a nursing home). Seriously, even though Ed has dark, wiry hairs that poke out of his nose, he's not half bad. He doesn't drool into his applesauce, forget his own name, or let his head loll off to one side like it's too heavy to hold up. You think I'm kidding about this stuff, but I've seen it pretty much daily, right here at good, ol' EHS.

Usually when I come, Ed has me push his wheelchair out to the far edge of the Everlasting's property, right up to the fence that runs next to the train tracks. We'll sit and wait for the 4:21 train to barrel through. While we wait, he'll ask me to list everything I've eaten since I last saw him. Like *everything*.

In detail. Once I almost forgot to tell him that I'd had grilled onions on my cheeseburger, and he launched into a five-minute lecture.

"Details, young man! What's life without all the little details to make it interesting? You young people today! You rush through everything. You're just like that granddaughter of mine. I have to tell Mel the same thing: Slow down! Smell the roses! Take a minute to enjoy what life has to offer, because before you know it you'll be old and hobbling around like me."

All that because I forgot onions. Sheesh.

Ed's diabetic and on this bland, sugarless diet, so I guess he lives through me and my stomach. It sucks for him, but I'm not allowed to bring him a candy bar or anything. Not that he doesn't beg me to. Like every time I come.

But earlier today, instead of being in his wheelchair ready to go, he was still in bed. Without even saying hello, he ordered me to close the door, shut the curtains, and not ask any questions. Weird. But then again, in the short time I've known him, Ed has occasionally done some odd stuff, like last week when he asked me to call this number for him; but as soon as the person answered, Ed just listened for a minute and then handed the phone back to me.

I should tell you—my mom would probably say this was important—that I'd had a rotten day. We'd been doing state testing in school, so my hand was cramped from filling in those stupid bubble sheets, and my head hurt from squinting while I tried to read all the questions. Track practice was cancelled after school because it was drizzling. Then, on my way out to my mom's car in the parking lot, Anthony Gutterson (a.k.a. The Gut) decided to yank my backpack off my back. Which snapped the strap, causing the whole bag to go flying into a nice little puddle. Yeah, I know, killer day, right?

So with Ed being all mysterious, and as cruddy as I was already feeling, I was tempted to bolt for the nearest exit. But then he started going on and on about this incredibly cool book he'd picked up back in 1943 when he was stationed at an air base in North Africa. Cue the mental eye roll. I figured this was Ed being Ed, trying to entertain me with his fabricated stories.

Here's the thing about Ed: I've known the old man for just a few weeks. In that short time, Ed has pulled his share of pranks, flirted with every nurse in the building, and told me such far-fetched stories that I've gotten used to just nodding and biting my tongue. Like when he told me that he'd once seen the inside of a whale's mouth. Or how he and Mel had run with the bulls in Pamplona, Spain, and were nearly gored to death but jumped to safety at the last minute. Or how he'd snuck up behind a Nazi soldier, asked him if he had a light for his cigarette, and then stabbed him with his butter knife. I've seen my fair share of war movies—*Schindler's List* and *Saving Private Ryan*—and nobody ever killed a Nazi with a butter knife.

But there was something about him today that seemed different. As he told me about this book, his eyes were animated, and his hands danced across its surface. He looked . . . well . . . he looked like he might just be telling the truth. For once.

"Wasn't till I got back to the States, Spencer my boy, that I figured out what this baby could do." Ed held up the book. Its plain blue cover was slightly faded. The letters that made up the title were large and embossed in gold but were peeling and barely visible. I could make out PAN, but the rest of the letters were too flaked off for me to see. No author. Ed held it up, his hands shaking. "*Pandora's Book*," he whispered reverently.

"Pandora? Isn't it 'Pandora's Box'? We read that myth last month," I said.

Ed shushed me with a wave of his hand.

"You know the story, then?" he asked, wheezing a little. "You know about Pandora and how she opened the box and—"

"All the evil in the world escaped, leaving hope trapped inside," I interrupted. "But it was a box."

"Box. Book. Doesn't matter. Think, boy, think," Ed said emphatically, squinting his watery eyes at me. "Think about the significance of that myth for mankind."

He was starting to sound like my English teacher.

And I'd had three hours of "read this passage and choose the correct answer" already today. I sighed deeply.

Ed shifted uncomfortably in his bed, wincing as his hip joints creaked like they needed to be oiled. He then cleared his throat, which—like it often did—morphed into a fit of coughing that racked his wafer-thin body.

As he laid the heavy book across his nearly useless legs and opened it up, something happened. There was a crackle in the room, as if a storm were coming or I'd rubbed a balloon on a fuzzy sweater. Automatically, I took a step away from his bed.

Ed's watery, yellowed eyes slowly slid up to find mine. "It's magic, boy. Magic."

He flipped a few pages. I already told you I'm blind as a bat, but from what I could tell, each page was filled with a picture, like the kind you'd find in a reference book. An encyclopedia maybe. But I couldn't tell who was pictured; he was turning the pages too fast. Then, suddenly, he stopped and smiled.

"Perfect," he said.

Excitedly, Ed grabbed what looked like a plain white bookmark that had been tucked into the back of the book. Starting from where the pages came together, he gently slid the bookmark across the page. Then he tapped his knobby fingers a few times on the surface of the picture and leaned back into the pillows stacked behind his head, his face expectant.

"Watch," he said softly.

For a second nothing happened. I was sure this was some kind of trick, another prank like last week's when he asked me to pour him some water from his pitcher and then laughed hysterically when the already-loosened lid popped off easily and I ended up drenched. But I was wrong. This was no trick.

I'll let you in on a little secret, too. What he was about to show me would change my life. And screw up my week in a big, big way.

CHAPTER 2
WHY I WAS HANGING OUT
AT AN OLD FOLKS' HOME

One minute, the room was quiet and empty—just me and Ed and the old ticking grandfather clock that he'd brought with him to the nursing home. The next minute? Babe Ruth was just all of a sudden *there*—his large belly straining against the buttons of his Yankees uniform. The Babe smiled broadly, leaned against his bat, and said, "Hiya, kid. Need some help with your ol' swing, now, eh?"

I was still standing at that point, but it felt like my knees were going to collapse. I think I blinked a few times. Maybe gasped. Kind of nodded, the way cartoon characters do when they're dumbstruck—mouth open, chin dropped, all bug-eyed.

Ed flipped a few more pages, slid the bookmark, did a little *tap-tap-tapping*, and *wallah*! We were joined by the weirdest-looking dude you've ever seen—his white-gray hair shooting every which way as if he'd just stuck a finger in a light socket. His eyes were full of mischief, like Ed's. His nose as big as a golf ball.

"So what do we have here?" Einstein asked, his eyes crinkling. He tucked his notebook in his back pocket, laced his fingers together, and brought both hands up to rest under his chin. "A young man struggling with numbers? Believe me, dear boy, whatever your difficulties with mathematics, I assure you mine are far greater."

Actually, math and I got along fairly well (though I couldn't say the same for my best friend, Gregor). But I wasn't going to tell that to the guy who created the theory of relativity and was a genius in subjects that started with words like *quantum* and *thermal*.

I looked quickly from Babe Ruth to Einstein to Ed. "How . . . ?" I shook my head as if I could knock the craziness right out of it. "Where . . . ? I mean, this is . . ."

Ed threw his head back and laughed. "But, wait, Spencer. I've saved the best for last."

He skipped forward to a page that I noticed had a dog-eared corner. Clearly, Ed had been here many times. Again, he slid the bookmark and tapped.

"Well, hello there," said the woman who appeared in our stuffy room. "Aren't you a handsome little devil?" And then Marilyn Monroe reached forward and kissed me on the cheek before I could move out of the way. I could feel the stickiness of her lipstick long after her lips had left my skin.

"You got some lady trouble?" she purred, smoothing out the front of her swirly white dress. She reached up to lightly pat her hair. "An adorable little fellow like you?"

That's when Ed told me who Marilyn Monroe was, then said, "Told ya, kid. It's the real deal," and I closed my eyes and fell back into the ratty, musty armchair that was Ed's favorite. I sneezed and had Babe Ruth bless me.

Now, through the thick lenses of my glasses, I looked at Ed, my eyes wide and disbelieving.

"How did you . . . ?" I choked out, feeling like I'd been socked in the gut.

Ed threw back his head and laughed like a giddy hyena. "I've waited so many years to show someone, Spencer. I knew you were the right choice the minute you first walked into my room."

For a second I just stared at him, thinking back suddenly to how much I'd wished that particular day hadn't happened at all, since it had never been my plan to spend my afternoons at a smelly nursing home with an old guy whose idea of fun was watching reruns of *Gilligan's Island.*

I have my mom to thank for all of this.

See, my mom is a firm believer in "giving back." Since the time I learned to walk and talk, I've tagged along (or more like been dragged along) on her volunteer missions, which often take us into the heart of Los Angeles—and not the pleasant, pink, frilly heart either.

I've served food at homeless shelters, walked 5Ks for cancer victims, brought books to children who are bald from chemo, and once spent a night on a cold street in South Los Angeles with my mom and sister so I could know what it was like not to have a bed every night. (FYI: My dad thought what my mom did was "honorable" and "selfless." But that night? He stayed home with the TV, his comfy mattress, and a meal that he could heat up in the microwave.)

Last month, I turned twelve. About time, my mom declared, that I start making my own difference in the world. I promised to save my allowance for four months and give it to AMVETS. I swore I'd clean out my closet and donate everything to the Salvation Army. I'd sign up for the next Relay for Life—the early morning shift even. But apparently, that wasn't what she had in mind.

I've got nothing against old people. Heck, my grandpa Tom is sixty-nine—which is pretty old, right? But even though my grandpa sometimes walks with a cane and hacks up a loogie every time he coughs, he'd be considered, like, youthful in this place. Seriously. These people are *old* old.

I begged my mom to let me do something else. Like deliver magazines to sick people at the hospital. Or walk Mrs. Agundez's dog, Horatio, who licked my ankles constantly and peed when you bent down to pet him. Or teach kids at the library how to use the computers. Or collect canned goods for the food pantry.

No dice. My mom knew some lady who worked in the administrative offices of the Everlasting Home for Seniors, and they were desperately looking for young people just like me, *blah, blah, blah* and *whatever, whatever, whatever.*

Which is how I ended up spending an hour twice a week—Tuesdays and Thursdays after track practice—getting my cheeks pinched and reading the newspaper to snoring, farting old men. Which is how I met Ed. And how I found out about *Pandora's Book.*

And why I was standing there holding a heavy wooden bat while Babe Ruth corrected my stance and gave me pointers on the perfect swing.

CHAPTER 3
I GET A GIFT . . . SORT OF

After a few minutes of batting practice, a quick demonstration from Einstein on how an object in motion stays in motion, and a weird (but okay, kinda nice) lesson from Miss Monroe on how to gently kiss a lady's hand, Ed looked toward Marilyn one more time with that stupid, loopy grin of his and then *tap-tap-tapped* them all back into their rightful pages—seconds before a nurse knocked on the door to announce it was time for Mr. Elofson's afternoon meds.

Ed smiled at the nurse who bustled into the room, bringing with her the scent of lavender and mashed potatoes. Though I'd been coming for a few weeks now, this was a new nurse—Nurse Margaret, Ed called her. She was older, maybe my mom's age, and had her hair twisted up in a tight braid that pulled at the corners of her eyes. I wondered if it gave her a headache.

"I see you have a visitor, Mr. E.," she remarked casually, glancing over at me. She held a paper cup full of water out to him and waited for him to swallow the three brightly colored pills she handed him. (Have you ever wondered why they make medicine look like candy? It doesn't taste like candy—why try to fool us?)

"This here's Spencer," Ed said, handing the empty cup back to her and opening his mouth wide so she could verify he'd swallowed them. "Good kid."

"Your grandson, then?" she asked pleasantly, moving over to the curtains and pulling them wide open to let in some afternoon light—what little was out there since it was overcast and drizzly. Obviously, Ed had asked me to close them before he'd pulled out *Pandora's Book*. His room was on the ground floor. Anyone walking by could have looked in and gotten the surprise of his life.

I was watching Ed's face closely. For half a

second—it was really that fast—his eyebrows tugged downward and his mouth pursed like he'd sucked on something sour. But he covered it quickly with a smile.

"Nope," he said lightly. "No grandkids." He winked at me. "Spencer's my new BFF."

I opened my mouth, but then I saw the look on his face and closed it. He talked about his granddaughter, Mel, constantly. All the crazy adventures they'd had. Why would he lie about her? Wouldn't they have records of these things? If Nurse Margaret wanted to, couldn't she find out exactly who Ed's family members were?

But then, so much about Ed was odd. Maybe Mel wasn't even real. He had no pictures of her up in his room. No pictures of any family, now that I looked around. Who didn't put up at least one picture of his family? A wife or some kids or something? Just one of many things about Ed that didn't quite add up.

The nurse, however, just gave Ed a look and laughed. She folded her arms across her ample chest and shook her head. "BFF. Hah! You've been watching too much Disney Channel, Mr. E. You tell

Spencer how much you like that show with the cute blonde girl who nobody knows is really a zombie?"

My sister, Molly, watched that show nonstop. On my "This Is Really Lame" scale, it was a ten. But somehow, it seemed like something Ed would enjoy. Mostly because the main character was hot.

The nurse headed toward the door. "You two behave in here."

Ed waggled his eyebrows at me behind her back. "Don't I always behave, Miss Margaret?"

Miss Margaret shook her head again as she disappeared.

I felt my shoulders sag and realized that I'd been stressing out the whole time she was in here. Worried, I guess, that she'd sense something weird had happened. Worried that Ed, who I still wasn't completely convinced wasn't off his rocker, would blurt out that we'd just hung out with Albert Einstein, and the nurse would think he was crazy and he'd be moved into lockdown and I'd never see him again. Which I realized at that moment would really bite. The guy was old, sure, but he was way cool.

"That was close, Ed." I leaned forward in my chair and put my elbows on my knees. "What if she'd walked in while they were, you know, here?" I gestured toward *Pandora's Book*.

Ed waved a gnarled hand in the air and harrumphed. "Margaret? Naw." He pointed at his old grandfather clock, which was always ticking away loudly in the corner. It was four forty-five. "She's like my morning bowel movement. As regular as they come."

I winced. Ed loved to talk about taking a dump. In fact, now that I thought about it, so did Grandpa Tom. Maybe it was an old-people thing.

Ed leaned back onto his pillows and ran his hand lightly over *Pandora's Book*.

"So?" he asked, not looking at me.

I leaned back in the armchair and tried to breathe through my mouth so I wouldn't inhale *eau de Ed*, otherwise known as mothballs, stale tobacco juice, and Bengay.

"So . . . what?"

"So how 'bout this little book of mine, huh?" He

grinned at me like a kid who'd just gotten a new video game.

"It's . . . amazing," I said. "How does it work?"

Ed shrugged. "Not sure. I won it in a poker game back during the war. Off this African shaman guy who wandered into the same bar I always went to when I was on leave. We were drinking so I don't remember much. But I do remember that he didn't look upset when he handed it over to me. More like . . . resigned maybe. I thought it was a worthless piece of crap at the time. Not really sure why I kept it. Somehow it made it back to the States with me, and found its way into my study." Ed looked out the window, lost in thought. "For years—decades, really—I didn't open it. Forgot I had it. Then, a few years back, Norma—my wife—passed on. Suddenly, I had plenty of lonely evenings to fill."

Ed paused for a second, and the room grew silent except for the ticking of his clock.

"It was summer of 2006, I think, when I came across this book again and opened it up one afternoon. I accidentally tapped my fingers on the page and wham, bam, thank you, ma'am! There she was. Julia Child. She was a chef, Spencer. Used to be on TV in the sixties and seventies. And there she was in my living room. Asking me if she could fix me up some sautéed pork chops and French Onion Soup."

I didn't know who Julia Child was, but I figured that A) she was dead—since that seemed to be the theme of this book, and B) she must have made killer good pork chops since people in this book all seemed to be experts at something.

"You can bet, kid, that I took her up on that. It was the best meal of my life. And I figured out pretty quickly that I could get them all—every single person in this book—to be at my beck and call. See, Spence"—he leaned closer to me and lowered his voice—"they're all here to serve you. Do whatever you need them to. You'll notice after a while that the first thing they ask when they pop out is how they can help you."

Help me.

Really. I closed my eyes, noting the darkness behind my eyelids, wondering how it would feel when that was all I saw, even when my eyes were open. If only they could help me.

I reached up and fingered my glasses—Coke bottles, Grandpa Tom called them. I couldn't remember a time when I didn't have to wear them. When my parents weren't worried about the disease that was sapping the sight from my eyes. *Retinitis pigmentosa.* A mouthful, huh? Dr. Burt said it could take years before I was legally blind. Probably, I'd be an adult. But there was no stopping it. And already, it was nearly impossible for me to see in the dark.

Ed coughed, and I pushed my glasses up my nose so I could see him better.

"Seriously, kid," Ed said and caressed the smooth blue cover of *Pandora's Book.* "It changed my life."

I believed him. It had changed mine and I'd just seen it for the first time about forty-five minutes ago.

"But, Ed, why did you show this to me? Why *me*?"

Ed's eyes grew serious. "Because you're the guy, Spencer. You're the guy who's supposed to take over for me. You're next, kid."

I felt my eyebrows dip. "I don't get it. What do you mean I'm next?"

"Don't you see? We don't choose *Pandora's Book*. It chooses us. I was a crappy poker player. I'd won a grand stinkin' total of half a dozen poker games in my life. I was drunk as a skunk. No way should I have beaten a shaman who had more wisdom, not to mention common sense, in his pinky than I did in my entire noggin." He tapped the side of his forehead. "I'll tell you something. The day before you walked into this room, trying to get away from the other crazy old farts here . . . the day before I met you, I had a dream. About *Pandora's Book*. It was floating around all willy-nilly, and I couldn't quite grab it. I tried and tried but these stupid, useless legs kept me anchored to this bed. The book drifted around like some kind of crazy daggone bird until the door to this very room opened. And in my dream, there was a flash of light, and the book was gone." He nodded as if this all made perfect sense to him. "You showed up the next day."

I stared at Ed. If I'd had any doubts that the guy was loony tunes before, this confirmed it.

"Why me?" I asked again. "What about Mel? Your granddaughter?"

I watched his face closely. Ed's eyes slid away from mine. He fingered the edges of the book for a second. Then he shook his head without looking up at me.

"Not Mel," he said slowly. "It's . . . No, Spencer. It's you. Of that, I'm sure."

He kept fingering the book. There was something he wasn't telling me.

"So," I said slowly, "you think *I'm* supposed to be the next owner of this book?"

I was pretty sure that Ed wasn't being completely honest with me, but even still, my skin prickled. Wow. There were some cool things I could do with that book. And what if . . . ? What if somebody in there *could* help me?

But Ed wouldn't look at me, and under his breath, I heard him chuckle. In that moment, I knew. He was going to tell me this was all a joke. One of his typical pranks. Maybe he'd gotten some of the staff members of the Everlasting to dress up as Einstein and Babe Ruth just to freak me out. I wouldn't put it past him.

"Look, Ed," I started and stood up. "If this is some kind of . . ."

"Spencer." His voice was commanding. Like I'd never heard it before. "Sit down, kid."

I sat.

"You're not just the owner, see?" He gazed down at the heavy book in his lap and back up at me. "You're more like the *guardian*—get me? A guardian of the past. You have some . . . er . . . responsibilities."

I waited. There had to be more. What kinds of responsibilities?

Ed didn't say anything for the longest time. He gazed at me seriously. He put a finger to his lips, sighed, opened his mouth, and closed it.

"Ed, really," I said after a minute or so. "I don't get what . . ."

There was a knock on the door. Nurse Margaret.

"Spencer, hon?" she said kindly when she stuck her head in the room. "Your mom is out front for you."

I glanced at the clock. Five o'clock on the nose. My mom is also about as regular as Ed's bowel movements. And she doesn't like to be kept waiting.

Nurse Margaret ducked back out. I stood up.

Ed inhaled deeply and dropped his eyes to *Pandora's Book*. Then, slowly, as if he wasn't sure he should, he held it out to me.

"Don't try to use it yet, okay? Not until I can teach you. This is heavy-duty stuff, Spencer. And like Pandora in that old myth, if we release it prematurely, we screw up everything, you hear? But look through it. Get familiar with who's in there. Take note of what their expertise is. And, Thursday, when you come back, bring it with you. We'll run through the dos and don'ts."

I reached toward him to take *Pandora's Book*. But Ed held on to it a second longer.

"Spencer," he said solemnly. Softly. And Ed is not a soft guy. Ever. I looked up at him. Met his watery brown eyes. Saw something there I couldn't quite name but that gave me a funny tickle in the pit of my belly. "Be careful. It's . . . important. For everyone."

He released the book, and I felt its full weight settle into my hands.

Maybe I should have been freaked out. Maybe I should have dumped that book in the first trash can I came to and told my mom I was done with the Everlasting Home for Seniors. Maybe I should have told someone about what had just happened.

Or just handed that book right back and said, "No way, uh-uh. I'm not cut out to be a guardian of the past or whatever. Can't you see I'm almost freakin' blind? Get somebody else to do it."

But I did none of those things. Instead, I took it home and showed it to my best friend, Gregor. Which was no doubt the worst thing I could have done.

CHAPTER 4

GREGOR MEETS SOCRATES

Gregor was pulled up into a tight ball on my bottom bunk, his kneecaps tucked under his chin. His fingers tapped frantically against his legs while his widened eyes darted between the book on my lap and the door. Not a good sign.

I was seriously wishing I'd never mentioned the stupid book to him.

"I know it sounds crazy, Gregor," I said for the third time. "But it really happened. I swear."

I sat cross-legged on the worn brown carpet floor of my room, the heavy blue book resting on my legs. I found myself running my hand over the cover, like I'd seen Ed do, wanting so badly to open it, but scared to at the same time.

"This is not a funny joke, Spencer," Gregor said in his nasally voice.

"It's not a joke, G." I sighed.

What was I thinking? Gregor has ASD—autism spectrum disorder. My mom explained to me once that this affected how Gregor communicates and hangs out with other people. Basically, it means that in about eighty percent of daily life, he's like every other sixth-grade kid. He goes to school with me, runs track, plays video games, and complains about homework. But it was the other twenty percent that I was worried about at the moment.

For example, this is the guy who goes ballistic if he has to wear a shirt with a tag. Who has to be practically sedated if Coach has us run a new route for cross-country practice. And I expected him to calmly accept that three dead people had popped out of a book and spoken to me? Gregor likes routine, predictability, calm. This had BAD IDEA written all over it.

"Listen," I said, standing up. "Let's forget about it, okay?" I started to walk over to put *Pandora's Book* on my desk. "Want to work on math homework or history first?"

I knew what Gregor would say. I asked this question every day. He answered the same way—every day. I was already reaching for my history book.

"I want to see it," Gregor said tonelessly. His eyes now darted from the book to me.

I froze, my hand grasping my history textbook. "What?"

"I want to see what's in the book, Spencer." His feet dropped to the floor, and his hands found their way to his thighs. His fingers kept tapping. Faster. "Come on, Spencer. Show me."

I glanced down at his tapping fingers. Both hands. Pinky to thumb and back again. A tapping Gregor was a soon-to-be-stressed-out Gregor. I fought the urge to start biting my thumbnail—an old habit I was desperately trying to break.

"But I can't . . ." I took a deep breath and grabbed the book. Then I spun toward Gregor. "I can't make it work yet. I don't know how. And Ed said not to mess around with it until he explains it. Dude, it's called *Pandora's Book*. How much more warning do you need?"

Gregor's tapping stopped. He looked thoughtful. No one knew Greek mythology like my friend. He was no doubt running through the entire story in his head. How Prometheus stole fire from the gods and gave it to man. And Zeus decided to punish Prometheus by making a clay figure of a smokin' hot chick which he then brought to life. The gods gave that lady, Pandora, all sorts of gifts like beauty, charm, wit, and curiosity. Then Zeus gave her a box, told her she was never to open it, and told Prometheus he could have this drop-dead gorgeous girl as a wife. Prometheus wasn't stupid; he knew it was a trick and said, "No way." Zeus got ticked off and punished Prometheus by chaining him to a rock and then let a vulture chow down on him. Prometheus's brother married Pandora, and the couple settled down for a happy life. But Pandora always wondered what was in the box Zeus gave her. Finally her curiosity won out. She opened the box, and out flew hate, anger, sickness, poverty, and every bad thing in the world. She slammed the lid down and managed to trap one final thing in the box: hope. So today, even when the going gets tough, every human still has hope.

No way could we let curiosity get the better of us. There had to be a really good reason this book was titled what it was. Especially after I had seen what it could do.

Gregor, however, wasn't giving up so easily.

"But he told you to look at it, right? To see who was in it?"

"Yeah." I nodded slowly. I sat next to Gregor. Before I knew it, I was chewing on my left thumbnail.

"We should look at the book, then, Spencer."

Ed *had* told me to look through it. He just said not to use it. So why did my stomach feel like it did when I was about to walk past Lilly Nelson, whose hair smelled like a strawberry smoothie but who didn't even know I existed?

Ignoring the uncertainty in my belly, I set *Pandora's Book* on my lap and opened the front cover.

Gregor leaned toward me, moving uncomfortably into my space, but without actually touching me. Sometimes he does that. I was used to it by now.

"It just looks like a book, Spencer," he said quietly.

He was right. It didn't look very remarkable, sitting there on my lap. My stomach calmed down a little. I flipped to the table of contents and leaned forward so I could see the words better. I began running my index finger down the list of names.

"Look, G.," I said, stopping my finger at about the fifth name on the list. "Leonardo da Vinci."

Gregor wiggled a little in excitement and pointed to another name farther down. I squinted to read it.

"Go to that one," he said eagerly. He quickly put his hand back on his leg. I saw his fingers twitch. He was working hard to stay cool.

Gregor might rock sometimes and do his tapping thing. And he really, really, really doesn't like surprises or anything out of his normal routine. Put him in a crowded place like Disneyland, and he either freezes or has a meltdown. But the guy loves history. Like, obsessively LOVES history.

One of my favorite things to do when I'm bored is to throw out a random date to Gregor.

"Dude. Sixteen ninety-eight."

Most of the time, Gregor doesn't even bother to look up from what he's doing. "A fire destroys the Palace of Whitehall in London. Zanzibar is captured by . . . Oman. And Peter I, a czar in Russia, imposes a tax on beards."

His ability to store facts about history is amazing. But the history he loves more than any other? Ancient Greece. Which is why it was no surprise that he was pointing to the twenty-third name on the list: Socrates, one of the greatest philosophers of all time.

I flipped to page twenty-three. It was indeed a picture of Socrates. Or a painting of him anyway. In it, Socrates was draped in a white sheet, though most of his chest was bare. He was sort of half lying, half sitting in a bed. One hand was raised in the air, his finger pointing upward. He looked a little irked, I thought. Like I would if Molly barreled into my room too early on a Saturday and woke me up.

Gregor's face screwed up in concentration while his mouth moved soundlessly through the words below the picture. Knowing him, though, he wasn't just reading them; he was memorizing them. Or whatever he did to make his brain suck up everything and remember it forever.

"Cool dude, that Socrates," I said and started to turn the page.

Gregor's palm smacked down on the book with a loud *thwack!* His eyes continued to roam over the painting.

"The people in this book can really come to life?" Gregor asked, his voice tight. "No joking?"

One tiny little butterfly started flapping its wings in my stomach.

"Well, that's what Ed said." I was really nervous with Gregor's hand on the image of Socrates. What if he tapped? What if . . . ?

"But you saw Einstein, right? And Babe Ruth? So you know it works?"

"Yeah, but Gregor," I said, "Ed told me not to try

it, remember? He said to wait until he could show me how to use it. Pandora and all that?"

I had to keep Gregor calm. If he started tapping ...

"Once I learn how it works on Thursday, we'll come back to this page," I promised. "First person we'll do is Socrates." I tried to slide the book out from under his hand, but he started pressing down too hard. I couldn't move it.

See, here's the thing: I've been Gregor's friend for almost three years. I know all of the little weird stuff he does. I know what sets him off. What calms him down. I know not to play my music too loud. I know he eats his lunch in the same order every day: fruit, sandwich, cookies, chips. I know that he wants to be on *Jeopardy* someday.

And I know he hates to be touched unexpectedly.

But sometimes? Even I forget.

I had to get that page out from under his hand before he started tapping. So I didn't think. I just reached out and tried to push Gregor's hand out of the way.

You need to understand that what he did next was instinctive. Not mean. Gregor has never been mean a day in his life. He doesn't know how.

Almost like he'd touched something burning hot, he yanked his wrist backward to shake off my hand. His elbow caught me right in the face, shoving my glasses against the bridge of my nose. The pain was instant, like someone had taken a frying pan to my face. I collapsed forward, both hands covering my throbbing nose.

"Dude!" I yelled.

I felt *Pandora's Book* slide sideways off my lap, but I was too busy trying to blink away the pain to care.

"Sorry, Spencer," Gregor muttered. "Really sorry, Spencer. I didn't mean to do that. I didn't mean to hurt you, Spencer."

And I knew he didn't. I *knew*. But knowing that didn't stop the pain.

I sat up and removed my glasses. My eyes were already watering. Closing them tightly, I rubbed the bridge of my nose and tried to massage away the pulsing ache that rocketed through my forehead and cheekbones. Gently, I set my glasses back on my nose and opened my eyes. I tried to blink away the tears that had formed.

My eyes cleared just in time to see Gregor lean forward.

"What's this?" he asked.

He held up the white bookmark. My breath caught.

"Gregor . . ." I had to keep calm but stop him. Pain still thumped in my temples. I reached for *Pandora's Book*.

Gregor slid the bookmark casually across the page. My stomach lurched.

I knew that look on his face. The widening of his eyes. The flush in his cheeks.

"No!"

But I was too late.

First the pinky finger. Then the ring finger. Middle finger. Index finger. Thumb. *Tap, tap, tap, tap, tap.*

There was a crackle. A heartbeat of stillness, like the world stopped turning.

And then . . . *poof.*

"Ah! Dear friends!" One hand came up to stroke his tangled beard. "*As for me, all I know is that I know nothing!* But maybe you would like help pondering a life of virtue versus a life of material wealth?"

Socrates was in my bedroom.

My mom was going to kill me.

Swallowing my panic, I looked over at Gregor, not knowing how he might react. When Gregor's circuit boards get too overwhelmed, he collapses in on himself. I call it "melting."

But Gregor wasn't melting. His eyes were wide and alert. Focused. His hands were no longer tapping. They were completely still.

"Spencer," he said, breaking into a wide, goofy grin. "This book rocks!"

Then—because you know in stories like this, everything always goes wrong—everything went wrong.

My mom's footsteps pounded down the hall.

"Spencer! Gregor!" she called. "When you guys want dinner?"

Her knuckles rapped lightly on my door. "Everything okay in there?"

Gregor freaked and lobbed the heavy book away from him as if it were on fire. The gigantic book, of course, landed on Socrates's bare foot. Socrates yelped loudly. Gregor covered his ears and winced in discomfort and confusion. I looked wildly from the closed bedroom door to Socrates, who danced on one foot (still yelping), to Gregor, who was rapidly on his way to melting. And I did the only thing I could think of.

I bolted.

CHAPTER 5
I FLASH BACK AND TELL YOU
HOW I MET GREGOR

I'm sure you turned the page hoping to find out where I ran off to and what happened to Gregor and Socrates. Well, you're going to have to hang on a minute, because I want to do what Miss Lipson, my English teacher, calls a *flashback*. I guess this is what real writers do when they want to fill the reader in on something that happened to the narrator (a.k.a. me) at an earlier point in time. Honestly, I usually skim over flashbacks in books because they're boring and they mess up the action. But this is my story, and I think it's pretty important that you know some stuff about me and Gregor before you read what happens next. Skip it if you want to.

(But I'll try to make it quick.)

My mom likes to say that I started running even when I was still in her womb. When she talks about stuff like that—me being in her WOMB—I get a little queasy. I mean, seriously, I understand that at one time, all of us were INSIDE our moms', you know, uterus. But it's just creepy. Why do moms say stuff like that anyway?

So when I was in fourth grade, my elementary school decided to organize a 2K race for all us kids to run in. It was supposed to be this big fund-raiser for our school, while at the same time encouraging health and fitness. But the top thing on my mind? First place in that race. I wanted to kick everyone's butts.

And I would have, too, if it weren't for Gregor.

Even though there were about two hundred kids and a handful of teachers running that day, I managed to wiggle my way up so that when the principal yelled, "Go!" through her megaphone, my toes were on that starting line, ready to fly. I knew I was faster than all of them. Even though we didn't officially have PE in fourth grade, we had to run around the playground a few times a week as a class, and

I always smoked everyone. There were a couple of decent runners in fifth grade, but they didn't understand how to win a race.

I did.

See, a 2K is about one and a quarter mile long. You come out too fast, and you're cooked by the half-mile mark. You come out too slow, and it's not a long enough race to make up lost ground. You have to stay calm and cool when everyone else bolts at the start. You have to save enough gas for the end. And you have to be able to push hard for the whole middle.

With just a quarter mile to go, there was only one kid in front of me. He was tall and olive-skinned, with short brown hair and long, measured strides. I couldn't see his face, but there was something about him that told me he was as focused and determined to win this race as I was. I couldn't let him do that.

As the seconds ticked by, I got madder and madder at this kid. Who did he think he was? Why had I never seen him before? I knew all the good runners at my school. Was he new? Had he been hiding out somewhere when we did those all-school morning runs? He wasn't going to take this away from me—no stinkin' way.

I pushed harder than I'd ever pushed before. My lungs were straining to keep up with my legs, which were burning like they never had. I was flying. As I rounded the corner of the school and got my first glimpse of the finish line, I caught up to him. We were neck and neck. I could hear his labored breaths, feel the air moving next to me as he ran. I pulled ahead by one foot, then two. But fast as lightning, he was shoulder to shoulder with me again.

The finish line was close now. People were cheering. Everyone likes a close race, and we were giving them one.

"Go, Spencer! Go!" I could hear my name being shouted over and over. I didn't hear any shouts for this other kid. Who was he?

I dug into what little energy I had left and floored it. For a second, I thought it was going to work. I pulled enough ahead to think I'd lost him. The finish line was only steps away. It was mine. In the bag.

But the other kid had some energy left, too. With

two strides left, he slid by me, leaning forward to beat me by half a second.

We both stood panting on the grass, bending over to stop the horrible feeling of the blood rushing back into our brains. I knew what I was supposed to do: say "nice race" and shake his hand. But, frankly, I was ticked off. This was MY race. I was supposed to win it. And when you're a skinny little kid with huge glasses, you need stuff like this to make it okay for kids to sit next to you at lunch.

But my mom was watching. The principal was watching. So I did the right thing.

I turned toward the guy and held out my sweaty hand. "Nice race."

The kid wouldn't look at me. And he didn't reach for my hand.

Instead, he started tapping his fingers on his thighs, while his eyes darted everywhere but at me.

"Nine minutes and nineteen seconds," he muttered to the ground, his voice monotone and nervous.

"What?"

I pulled my hand back awkwardly and slid my

glasses up my nose. Then I started chewing on my sweaty thumb.

"Nine minutes and nineteen seconds," he repeated.

"Yeah, okay, whatever," I said, wiping my thumb on my shirt. I started to walk away.

But then I heard him say, "You run really fast. Like Pheidippides."

Not many kids my age knew about Pheidippides. The first guy to ever run a marathon. Back in ancient Greece in 490 BC. But my dad used to read me this story about him. It was, and still is, one of my favorites.

I slowly turned around.

"What did you say?"

The kid started rattling off facts like he was Wikipedia. In a flat tone, he said really quickly, "Pheidippides was an Athenian herald. He was sent to Sparta to get help when the Persians showed up at Marathon, Greece. He then ran twenty-six miles from a battlefield near Marathon to Athens to announce that the Greeks had beaten Persia."

My jaw dropped.

"What's your name?" I asked.

He still wouldn't look directly at me. His hands were tapping like crazy.

"Gregor."

"Do you go to school here?"

His eyes snuck their way up to mine, even though his chin stayed firmly on his chest. He didn't answer.

"You ran a really good race," I said begrudgingly.

"Nine minutes and nineteen seconds," he said, and for the first time, his head popped up and he looked at me. Not right in the eyes, though. Kind of around me.

"You timed it?"

He held up his watch proudly. "Last week, nine minutes and twenty-five seconds. Today, nine minutes and nineteen seconds."

This kid was truly weird. But there was something about him that kind of fascinated me, too. Plus, he was a runner. A good runner. That counts in my book.

I didn't see Gregor for the next couple of weeks at school and believe me, I was looking. I started to think he was some middle-school kid who'd snuck into the race. Or maybe he was homeschooled and didn't want anyone to know.

Then one day my teacher asked me to deliver a note to the office. And there he was, sitting in one of the chairs that kids sit in when they're sick and have to be picked up to go home. Gregor didn't look sick. He looked scared to death.

"Gregor?" I said to him after I handed my note to the secretary.

Gregor didn't look up. He had his knees pulled up to his chest, his eyes closed, and was humming tonelessly under his breath. His fingers were tapping against his legs.

"Hey, Gregor," I said a little louder. Gregor still didn't move.

The secretary, however, rushed over.

"Don't mind him, hon," she said to me, as if Gregor couldn't hear us. "He gets like this sometimes. We just leave him alone until he comes out of it."

Something didn't seem right about all this. I'd talked to Gregor after the race that day. And though he seemed . . . well, a little odd, he didn't seem like a bad kid or someone who deserved to be talked about like he wasn't in the room.

I ignored her.

"Yo, Gregor," I said and sat down carefully in the chair next to him. "You run that 2K course lately?"

Gregor stopped humming. His tapping slowed. He didn't look at me.

"Nine minutes and sixteen seconds," he said quietly in his flat voice.

"Really? That's awesome," I said casually. "A new personal best for you. Maybe you could run with me after school today. You could, like, pace me or something."

Gregor's death grip on his knees loosened. "Like Pheidippides."

I laughed. "Yeah, like Pheidippides."

The secretary was looking at us with equal parts suspicion and fascination.

I started to stand up.

Gregor's voice, clearer now, stopped me. "What's your name?"

I smiled and turned toward him. "My name is Spencer."

While the secretary stared, Gregor completely uncurled himself. He raised his eyes to mine. "Spencer." A slow smile spread across his face. "But I will call you Koroibos, the first Olympic champion in the *stadion* race."

I laughed again, loudly this time. "Cool. And I'll call you Pheidippides?"

Gregor smiled broadly. "Yes. Pheidippides."

Gregor and I started running together every day after school, and we've been friends ever since. Not everybody understands it; in fact, Gregor makes a lot of people uncomfortable. But that's something I grew to really like about him—he's unpredictable and yet extremely predictable all at the same time. And he's the only person who can kick my butt in a footrace. Just like I'm the only person who can sometimes kick his.

Okay, so now you know how Gregor and I met. Flashback over. Wasn't so bad, was it?

I now return you to your regularly scheduled story. Unless you skipped this chapter, like I probably would have. In either case, turn the page if you want to know who showed up on my doorstep and how we managed to lose Socrates.

CHAPTER 6
WE GET AN
UNEXPECTED VISITOR

With Socrates howling and Gregor in a partial meltdown, I had to cut my mom off or she was going to walk in, freak out, and I'd probably be grounded until I was Ed's age. Which would suck.

So I quickly squeezed out my bedroom door, closing it firmly behind me, and met her in the hallway.

Her eyes made it clear that she was in CSI-Mom mode. Not good.

"What's going on in there, Spencer?" she asked, looking past me at my closed bedroom door. Socrates's yelps had just stopped and even Gregor was (thankfully) quiet.

"My . . . um . . . alarm on my phone went off accidentally, and it freaked Gregor out," I said, trying not to look at Mom. She has this radar thing where she can look in my eyes and tell instantly when I'm lying. It's scary, actually. "You know how he hates loud noises."

"Maybe I should make sure he's okay." She reached for the doorknob.

I moved so I was blocking her way.

"No, Mom!" I swallowed and looked up at her, trying to keep my expression, well, expressionless. "Lately, he's . . . uh . . . embarrassed when people see him like this. Just . . . is, like, dinner almost ready?"

My mom's eyes did that squinty thing that lets me know she isn't convinced.

"You're sure I shouldn't go check on him?"

"Totally sure, Mom." I leaned my ear toward the door. "See? He's already calmed down. We're good, Mom. Seriously."

She sighed and took a step backward. "All right, then. You go deal with Gregor, and I'll heat up the lasagna."

It was Tuesday, which meant Gregor had dinner with us while his mom worked the late shift. It also meant we had lasagna because that's what Gregor always eats for dinner on Tuesdays. Always.

"Great, Mom. Awesome. Thanks."

I ducked back into my bedroom and closed the door firmly. We had maybe twenty minutes until dinner would be ready. We needed to get Socrates back in *Pandora's Book*. ASAP.

Which, judging by the scene before me, was going to be like asking Anthony "The Gut" Gutterson to wear a tutu and dance in the talent show.

Gregor sat on my bed, both feet flat on the floor, his eyes all bright and excited. His hands were calm and pressed firmly into his thighs. Socrates sat at my desk stroking his beard, his legs crossed casually under his toga.

"The most important possession a human can have is virtue, dear boy," Socrates said. "And, of course, there can be no greater virtue than one that is philosophical or intellectual."

Gregor leaned forward. "We should value virtue,

which is really knowledge, above all else," he said eagerly, his voice rising. "You always taught that life should be spent in search of good."

"Yes! Yes!" Socrates declared, his voice rising. "And what of the job of the philosopher?"

"To point out how little we all actually know."

"Dear boy!" Socrates smiled broadly and clapped his hands. "You have the makings of a fine thinker!"

Gregor glowed.

My shoulders slumped. No way was Gregor going to let me break up this once-in-a-lifetime chat with his idol so I could send Socrates back to being a lifeless picture in a book.

Unless . . .

"Yo, Gregor," I said casually. "My mom's making dinner. Should be ready in a few minutes."

I knew what he'd say next. It never failed.

His eyes twitched. "It's lasagna. Right, Spencer? Tuesday is lasagna."

"Oh, snap!" I slapped my fist to my forehead. "I think she forgot, dude!" His eyes widened. "I could have sworn she said something about tacos."

"But Tuesday is lasagna day. It's always lasagna day."

I sighed dramatically. "You better run out and tell her, man. Quickly."

Gregor shot a worried glance at Socrates and then looked toward my bedroom door. He was torn. Socrates? Or Taco Tuesday?

Gregor stood up. "I'll be right back, Spencer. I'll hurry. Don't do anything, okay?"

I nodded vaguely as he jetted out the door.

I grabbed the book and the bookmark and frantically flipped to the page—now blank—that Socrates was supposed to be on. I shoved my glasses up my nose. How did Ed do this? Maybe the same way he got these people here but in reverse?

I tapped on the page, slid the bookmark, glanced at Socrates, gritted my teeth in frustration, tapped some more, slid some more, and then flopped backward onto my bed in defeat. I chewed on my thumbnail. Socrates still regarded me passively. And Ed was going to kill me.

"Perhaps there is some way I can be of assistance?" Socrates's voice was gentle.

I looked up at the man I'd only ever seen in my sixth-grade history book. "Maybe you know how to jump back into this book," I said hopefully.

Socrates smiled wryly. "Alas, I simply come when called. I know not the ways of this world."

Something he said made me pause. "You're real, then? Not just a hologram or a technological trick or something? You're the real Socrates."

He chuckled. "I am, indeed." He held up his slightly hairy bare arm as if to prove he was real. I felt my lip curl a little in disgust—these Greek dudes weren't exactly known for their cleanliness.

"You didn't mean to summon me, then?" he asked.

I shook my head. "I just got this book today. The guy who had it before me—Ed—said to wait until he could show me how to use it. But then Gregor got all excited and . . ." I let my words trail off.

"Gregor's your friend?"

I nodded.

"He has a remarkable mind."

I chortled. He had no idea.

"So your problem is how to get me back to where I belong."

I nodded again.

Socrates stroked his beard, which I was learning meant that he was about to say something really wise but not really helpful. *"The only true wisdom is in knowing you know nothing."* His eyes sparkled.

(Called that one, didn't I?)

I stood up and walked over to my window, which looked out onto the pool in our backyard. A pool that badly needed somebody to clean it. Sometimes, though, if I stared into the barely rippling water, I could think.

The rain had mostly stopped, but heavy, gray clouds still blanketed the sky. The water in the pool rippled slightly as random droplets plinked on its surface. Something about that water mellowed me out and let my mind do what it needed to do.

I had a couple of options. Plan A: do nothing, let my mom completely freak out when she found a guy in a toga in my room, tell her the truth, and watch her freak out again. But then she would probably call the nursing home to talk to Ed or even take me down there, and I might get some answers from him on what to do. The problem with that scenario, besides the massive freaking out, was that it meant letting the secret of *Pandora's Book* out of the bag. And somehow, I didn't think that was a good idea.

Plan B: Look up the nursing home's number online, call Ed, and have him walk me through the process of putting Socrates back. Bingo!

I was bending over to dig my cell phone out of my backpack when the turning of my bedroom doorknob made me jump.

"Hold on!" I hollered, my heart hammering, in case it was my mom.

Gregor's wide blue eyes popped open as he peered around the edge of the door. "Hold on to what? My horses?" Then he laughed hysterically at his own joke and came into my room.

"You could have knocked, you know," I said and flashed him a nasty look.

Gregor smiled easily. "She remembered. It's lasagna." Then he turned toward Socrates, and they were once again lost in some philosophical mumbo jumbo about ignorance, virtue, and how you can tell if cheese is really good. Sheesh.

I'd just managed to find the number for the Everlasting Home for Seniors when I heard the doorbell ring. I glanced at my alarm clock next to my bed. Six-fifteen. Gregor's mom—a dentist who works long hours—didn't usually come get him until about seven or so. With a mental shrug—it was probably only a delivery guy or somebody trying to sell us new windows—I hit the Call button on my phone, hoping they would put me through to Ed's room quickly.

A pleasant voice on the other end said, "Good evening. Everlasting Home for Seniors. How may I direct your call?"

I cleared my throat and tried to sound older. "Uh, yes. I'm looking for Ed Elofson, please. I believe he's in room thirteen."

"Just a moment, and I'll connect you."

I was breathing a huge sigh of relief that this

would all be cleared up soon, when my mom hollered at me from down the hallway.

"Spencer! Somebody's here to see you."

Gregor's eyes met mine. We were both thinking the same thing. Someone to see me? Weird. I wasn't exactly in the popular group at school. My friend list extends pretty much to . . . well, Gregor, and a couple of guys on the track team. I told you, people get a little weirded out by Gregor so we keep our circle of friends small. Really small.

I raised my eyebrows at him and handed him my cell phone. "If Ed comes on the line, just tell him that Spencer needs to talk to him, okay? Tell him I'll be right back."

I slipped out of my bedroom and padded down the hall.

My mom stood in our entryway, with one hand on the door. She was looking at whoever was on our front porch with her Statue of Liberty look.

My heart took a nose dive.

My mom has a thing for people—damaged, lost,

homeless, hungry, needy—you name it. She's like the Statue of Liberty for our neighborhood. You know: "Give us your tired, your poor, your huddled masses."

Apparently, the latest "huddled mass" had just arrived on our doorstep. Except he was a kind of overweight dude in a dirty overcoat, funny hat, and way outdated shoes, and he really looked like he needed a nap, a shower, and some lasagna.

"Maybe you'd like to come in for a second," my mom said pleasantly. Before long, he'd be at our table, heaping lasagna on his plate, wrapped in one of my dad's old robes. Oh, believe me—I'd seen it happen before.

I was about to make a beeline back to my room, figuring there was no way this guy was here to see me, when two things happened at the same time.

First, Gregor came running down the hallway holding my phone out. "Spencer!" he said, his eyes wild. "I gotta tell you something!"

But it was the second thing that made my blood run cold.

The guy on the front porch locked eyes with me. And I knew in that second that he was there for me, and he knew exactly who I was.

Then he moved his arm ever so slightly, so I could see that he was holding something. It was a slim book. With a blue cover. Similar to the one Ed had given me, but much smaller. It was titled simply *Pandora's Other Book.*

CHAPTER 7
THE DUDE IN THE TRENCH COAT CREEPS US OUT AND WE LOSE SOCRATES

You're Spencer Lemon?"

The guy on the porch was pudgy with a round face, bushy eyebrows, and large, bulgy eyes. His faded black trench coat and gray fedora made him seem slightly menacing despite his babyish, rosy-red cheeks and full lips. A brown, droopy cigar hung from the left side of his mouth. He wasn't smiling. But he wasn't glaring either.

"It's Le-MONE. Not like the sour fruit."

I had yet to meet someone who pronounced my last name correctly. Even my math teacher, Mr. Martinet, screwed it up. And he was, like, real-live French.

"You're da guy, then?" He shook his head and

looked down at the cell phone in his hand. "For Chrissake, you got a kid, Eddie? This is a bad idea."

The guy sounded gangster. But despite being such a big dude, his voice was soft and raspy.

My mom placed her hand on my shoulder. "You know this man, Spencer?"

I shook my head. My palms were sweaty, though.

"He don't know me," the guy said and jammed his phone in the pocket of his trench coat. "But I got a message for him. From Eddie."

My eyes widened, and I looked back at Gregor. He was standing rock-solid still at the corner where our hallway dumped out into our entryway.

"I gotta talk to you, Spencer," he muttered.

I held up one finger and swung my head back toward the guy on the porch. "You know Ed?"

The guy guffawed. "Sure, I know Eddie. We been playing poker every Tuesday night since I's can remember."

Poker.

I looked down at the book in the guy's hands.

"Where'd you get that?" I asked, squinting to try to make out if there was any other writing on the cover. There was nothing that I could see. Just *Pandora's Other Book*. In embossed gold letters.

I could see the guy's fingers tighten around the book.

"Listen, Spencer," he said, nervously glancing from me to my mom to Gregor. "You and me gotta talk. About that little, uh, gift that Eddie gave you today."

I could see my mom waver. Part of her—her Statue of Liberty part—still wanted to welcome this guy to our table, clean him up, and send him on his way with a few bucks and a new toothbrush (she has a drawer of them for occasions just like this). The other part—the Mama Bear part—was starting to worry about our safety.

"I'm sorry, but I think you'll have to come back later when my husband's home." My mom fingered her ponytail nervously. "We'd, uh, be happy to help you then."

The guy started digging around in one of his trench coat pockets and for a minute, we all stepped back. There was no telling what he would pull out. A gun. A knife. Moldy cheese.

But instead, his pudgy fingers pulled out a small, rectangular card which he held out to me.

"Things are going to get crazy, Spencer Lemon," he said, his eyes boring into mine. He'd said my name with a perfect accent.

I don't know why I did it, but I reached out and took the card. And I noticed then that even though the guy looked like he'd crawled out of the sewer, his hands were smooth and his fingernails clean and neatly trimmed.

"You call me, you hear?" he said and backed up a few steps. "I got answers."

And then he spun around and lumbered down the short walkway to a beat-up VW bug. Its pink exterior was scratched, dented, and rusted in some places. A large purple peace sign had been spray-painted on the passenger side door. It took him three tries before the engine caught, and when it did, he roared up the block and out of sight without even glancing back at the three of us, who stood at the front door, stunned.

My mom slowly closed the door and, arms crossed over her chest, turned to face me.

"Want to tell me what that was all about?" she said, with a look that left no doubt what might happen if I didn't.

"Honest, Mom," I said, looking right into her eyes. "I have no clue. Ed's the guy I go see at the nursing home on Tuesdays and Thursdays." I looked down at the card in my hand.

"Frank DiCarlo, Broker," I read off the card. There was a phone number and a web address.

My mom snatched the card from my hands. "I think we need to tell your dad about this and let him handle it." Her eyes darted down at her watch. My dad was working late that night. "Should we call the police, do you think? They might be able to pick him up and take him to one of the local shelters." She started biting the cuticles of her thumb. Like mother, like son.

A few things flashed through my mind at that moment. Ed handing me *Pandora's Book*. DiCarlo saying that things were going to get crazy and that he had answers. And Socrates saying that the only true wisdom was in knowing you knew nothing.

And that's when I remembered Socrates was still in my bedroom. The police were *definitely* a bad idea.

"No, Mom," I said hastily. "I'm sure Dad can handle it when he gets home. I mean, the guy didn't try to come in or anything, and he left when you told him to. He didn't look all that scary, anyway. Just . . . dirty."

My mom was still gnawing on her cuticle. "But he knew your name, Spencer. It was creepy." She quit chewing on herself. "I'm calling your dad."

It wasn't great, but it was better than the police. At least it gave us time to solve the Socrates problem.

"Okay, then," I said and started backing toward Gregor. "We're going to go finish up our homework. We don't have much since there was testing today. Cool?"

She looked at her watch again. "Molly'll be dropped off from dance in about fifteen minutes. We'll eat then, so be ready." And then she spun on her heel, probably to find her cell phone and call my father.

Careful not to touch him, I herded Gregor down the hall toward my room.

"Spencer, I have to tell you something." His voice was urgent.

"Dude," I whispered. "We've got to hide Socrates or something, like, ASAP. After what just happened, my mom's not going to . . ."

Gregor stopped so abruptly I crashed into him.

"Dude!" I yelped accusingly.

"Spencer," he half whispered, turning his head so I could see his wide eyes. "I closed the door. I swear I closed the door."

I squeezed past him and saw what he was talking about. The door to my room was partially open. I quickly pushed the door the rest of the way open and froze.

"Socrates?" I called out softly.

No one answered. My room was empty.

Gregor eased into the room behind me and stopped. He tipped his head sideways and looked thoughtful. "Maybe we don't have to hide Socrates after all, Spencer. Maybe he hid himself."

My stomach felt like I was on the Tower of Terror ride at the California Adventure theme park. And I was screaming toward the ground at one hundred miles per hour.

I launched myself at my bed and grabbed *Pandora's Book*.

"Please, please, please," I mumbled as I flipped pages as fast as I could.

Page twenty-three.

My heart stopped.

It was blank. Wherever Socrates was, he wasn't back in this book.

"Spencer," Gregor said with urgency in his voice. "Listen to me."

I looked up at my best friend.

"I talked to the lady at the nursing home, Spencer. Ed's missing."

CHAPTER 8
I GET A MESSAGE
FROM ED

When Gregor went home that night, we still hadn't found Socrates. Believe me, we'd tried. We'd figured that he must have wandered out, worked his way into my parents' bedroom, and slipped through their sliding glass door into our backyard. Where he went from there was anyone's guess. We ran up and down the streets for a few minutes, calling for him. A guy in a toga should be easy to spot, right? Yeah, no.

I hoped wherever he was, he was okay. Even though it was April in Southern California, it was still pretty chilly at night. A guy wearing a sheet was bound to get a little cold wandering around the city after dark.

You might think that knowing I'd let Socrates loose in my city would have topped my list of problems, but it didn't. I had other things to worry about. *Big* things.

Ed was, indeed, missing. I called the nursing home again and had the lady on the phone confirm what Gregor had already told me: Ed had disappeared. They'd gone in to get him for dinner and found the room completely empty. Hugely weird, since Ed couldn't walk well on his own anymore. I told her who I was and how I knew him. From there, the conversation got even weirder.

"Wait, you're Spencer Lemon."

"Le-MONE," I corrected, with years of practiced patience under my belt.

"We found something in the room for you."

I sat up straighter, mentally scrolling through the possibilities. Had I forgotten something there? Was there *another* book with crazy powers? Maybe he'd left me a clue?

"For me? What? What is it?"

"Hold on." I heard her set the phone down, while

I tried to breathe normally and not bite my thumbnail down to a bloody mess. What in the world could he have left me? I glanced over at *Pandora's Book*, sitting on my desk. Was there more? Was there a warning? Instructions on how to use it? Something to protect myself with now that I was the Guardian or whatever?

I heard a click as the lady at the nursing home picked up the phone.

"It's an envelope, hon," she said. "With your name on it."

"Where . . ." I gulped. "Where did you find it?"

"I think they found it under his pillow. Do you want to come down and get it, hon?" She paused. When she spoke again, her voice was quieter. "I'm guessing the police will be involved here quickly. We've tried contacting his family, but all the numbers on his forms . . . they're wrong numbers. We're trying to track down who's been paying for him to stay here. Nobody's ever heard of an Ed Elofson. It's really strange, you know? So what I'm saying is, if you want this, maybe you'd better . . ."

I got it. If the police came, this would be evidence, and they'd grab it. I may never know what it said.

"Can you open it?" I asked. "And read it to me?"

I was taking a risk. If it said something about the book, she was going to get really suspicious. On the other hand, I wasn't going to be at the Everlasting Home for Seniors again until Thursday. I couldn't wait that long.

"Sure," she said brightly. I heard her rip into the envelope. "Well, it looks like it's just a small piece of paper. Hmmm . . . that's strange."

I wanted to scream at her to just read it and quit the commentary. My poor thumb had literally no nail left.

"It doesn't say much, Spencer honey. But maybe it means something to you."

"What?" I asked impatiently. "What does it say?"

"It just says 'Find Mel.'" She paused to let that sink in. "You know who Mel is?"

I fell back against the pillow of my bed and closed my eyes.

Mel. Find Mel. *Oh, Ed. You've got to be kidding.*

I thanked the lady and hung up, my mind spinning.

Find Mel. Was she even a real person? In front of the nurse, Ed had acted as if she didn't exist. I certainly had no idea how to go about finding her. Did she live close by? How old was she? Was her last name Elofson? My head spun with the overwhelming possibilities.

But Mel wasn't the only person on my brain as I tried to focus on my homework that night.

There was also the little issue of Frank DiCarlo. I did a Google Search on his name and found that a Frank DiCarlo lived in New York and was wanted by the FBI for things like tax evasion, mail fraud, and embezzlement. Another Frank DiCarlo was a chef in Chicago. A third one had just gotten married for the fifth time in Boca Raton. None of them seemed to be the guy who had shown up at my front door.

My dad had been concerned enough to alert the police when he got home. Two stern-looking officers showed up, but other than asking a few questions, dropping the business card in a plastic baggie as evidence, and reminding us to keep our doors and windows locked that night, they didn't seem all that worried. I was tempted to ask them if they'd had any reports of a toga-wearing guy with a beard wandering around the neighborhood. But my parents were in the room and I thought it might sound a little suspicious.

Later that evening, my parents settled down to watch some show they liked about people who collected way too much stuff and then had to have, like, an intervention or something. I excused myself to my room, saying I still had to do homework, which was actually true.

For a few minutes, I just lay down on my bottom bunk, trying to make sense of the day. I felt a tiredness building behind my eyes and a tightness there that sometimes happened when I was stressed. It was the disease, I knew. The stupid disease that was destroying my retina and that was probably going to leave me legally blind at some point, though when, no one knew. No cure. No remedies. Just, hey, kid, good chance you'll lose your night vision, then your peripheral vision, then poof! One day, the whole kit and caboodle.

I took off my glasses, set them on the small table by my bed, and closed my eyes. It felt good to just lie there a moment, even though my brain was in overdrive. Through the thin wall that separated our rooms, I could hear Molly singing along to a song only she could hear through her iPod. She was happily belting it out, probably working on her third-grade homework—which was usually a math sheet and some reading. I sighed. Even though we'd had testing today, I still had a whole page of equations to solve and a paragraph to write for history. And I knew I should probably spend a few minutes practicing my violin for our upcoming end-of-the-year concert.

But I couldn't concentrate on any of it.

Everything that had happened since I'd walked into Ed's room at four o'clock that afternoon had just been so incredibly strange. And it all seemed to revolve around *Pandora's Book*. I didn't think that Ed's disappearance was just a coincidence.

The question was: Had he left on his own? Or had someone taken him? That last thought left a hollow feeling in my stomach. If someone had taken him, who? DiCarlo? But why? And what did Mel have to do with it all?

I put my glasses back on, swung my feet off my bed, and hurriedly rushed over to grab *Pandora's Book* from my desk. I tapped on the bright reading light that I needed to see at night, flopped on my bed, and flipped to the table of contents, skimming over the list of names, trying to see if there were any clues about Ed or Frank DiCarlo there. Franklin Delano Roosevelt. Julius Caesar. Einstein. Leonardo da Vinci. Even Walt Disney. Elvis Presley. Mother Teresa. And Michael Jackson. All people I would have really enjoyed meeting. But nothing clued me in to where Ed had vanished to, or who Frank DiCarlo was.

But I did notice something else. The people in this book were all what my history teacher would have called "notable figures." They'd all made some kind of significant impact on society—in a positive way. Some were inventors. Others were leaders. Others still were artists. The peeps in this book were all well loved, or at least respected. The good guys. I wasn't sure how that fit with Pandora's story. All the things in her box were evil.

The magical white bookmark was still tucked near the blank page where Socrates should have been. A full-color photo of Martin Luther King Jr. sat on the facing page. Apparently, there was no particular rhyme or reason to how the people were ordered—not chronologically or alphabetically, for sure.

I was hoping that maybe something near the back of the book might give me a clue about how it worked or how I might get Socrates back into it, if he ever turned up. But there was nothing there. Just a blank white page. I wondered, if someone famous died, did he or she automatically turn up in *Pandora's Book*? Or did I have to do something to get them in there?

I closed the book with a loud *thud*. Without Ed,

I might never know. And since, like that stupid Pandora, I had royally screwed up with Socrates, I wasn't all that eager to experiment.

I needed to find Ed and give the book back. I was the wrong guy for this job. Guardian or whatever he'd said. At some point in my future I'd probably be mostly, if not completely, blind. What good was a blind kid going to be as keeper of an important book like this? I also had zero skills when it came to defending even my own self. Case in point: My best defensive move against Anthony Gutterson? Avoiding him.

No, I thought with certainty, this kind of stuff is way out of my league.

Eventually I dug into my homework like I'd promised my parents, though I can't say I was really focused. Fortunately, math is easy for me—though I hoped Gregor was doing okay. With all the craziness of the afternoon, he'd left before we'd gotten anything done. He was a genius when it came to history, but he sucked at math. He'd told me once that it was like the numbers just floated around on the page, mocking him. Dates he's good with. But add a plus or equal sign and it wigs him out.

By nine o'clock, my homework was done. I promised myself I'd practice violin the next day. Then my mom came in to make sure I said my prayers—something she's done every night since I stopped sleeping in a crib.

"Keep Grandpa Tom and Auntie Debi healthy," I said to my blurry folded hands, since my mom insisted I take my glasses off to pray. "And watch over all the starving children of the world."

For a second, the room was silent. This was usually where I said my "amen," and my mom would stand up, tell me she was proud of me, and turn off the light. But tonight, another request nagged at me from the back corners of my brain.

"And Lord," I said and cleared my throat. "Help those who are, uh, missing find their way back home. Soon." I squeezed my eyes closed for emphasis. And muttered an amen.

When my mom left and my room was dark, I lay in bed trying not to worry about the things I couldn't control, like my Grandpa Tom often reminded me to do. But worry, I think, is like a mosquito bite: the more you try not to think about it, the more it consumes you. Until all you're left with is a scratched-up, bloody mess.

CHAPTER 9
WE GET A SURPRISE AT LUNCH

e had state testing again the following day at school, so for the whole morning I was confined to the library with my number-two pencil, a Scantron answer sheet, and about forty other kids who, like me, were in agony by lunchtime. The good news was that, because of the testing schedule, we had just one short test after lunch and then we got to leave early.

I found Gregor sitting in our usual spot on a low concrete wall that ran along the edge of the outside lunch area, tap-tap-tapping his fingers against his thighs, his lunch spread out but untouched beside him. Not good.

"You okay, man?" I slid next to him and pulled

out the brown bag that was squished between *Pandora's Book* (which I figured was safer with me than anywhere else) and my track shoes. It was sunny today, which meant after-school practice would not be cancelled. That was good, at least. I needed the distraction.

Gregor didn't answer, but he tentatively reached out for one of the three orange segments his mom packed him. That was normal, at least. Gregor always ate his fruit first.

I'd told Gregor about my conversation with the lady at the nursing home. He didn't think we should look for Mel at all. He thought we should just let the police handle everything. I wasn't too sure. How were we going to explain that there was a guy in a toga running around who was our responsibility? And though I really wanted to get this book out of my possession and back in Ed's hands as soon as possible, I felt an obligation to try to protect it while I had it. Which meant keeping it secret.

I pulled out a smooshed and soggy peanut butter and jelly. No matter how many times I've asked my mom to put peanut butter on both pieces of bread before she spread the jelly, she never remembers. So the jelly made the bread all wet and gross. But it was all I had. Plus, there were kids starving in Africa, right? I should know since I donate half my allowance to them every month.

"You make it through the math test stuff okay?" I said through a mouthful of sandwich.

Gregor stayed silent as he sucked his orange segment dry. His other hand was still tapping, though a little less frantically.

I watched Gregor reach for a second orange slice. When it was completely void of juice and all that was left was the thin, stringy membrane that held the fruit together, Gregor set it down and looked up at me.

Gregor has the lightest blue eyes I've ever seen on a human being, especially one who is half-Indian. So light, they almost look translucent. And when he's wide-eyed and upset, like he was at that moment, they can look a little creepy. Like maybe he was a vampire in another life or something. Seeing how well he can suck the life out of an orange, I have to wonder.

"What's going on, Gregor?" I asked softly. "What happened?"

"He's here, Spencer," Gregor said.

My mind flashed back to the night before.

"Who? Socrates?" I looked around quickly, but didn't spot an old guy in a white toga. Then another thought hit me, and my heartbeat quickened. "Ed? Was Ed here?"

I kept my voice low, but it wasn't necessary. Other kids didn't eat near us.

Gregor shook his head.

"Look across the street, Spencer. Near the corner."

Just a few feet behind us was a chain-link fence that wound around the entire campus. Beyond that was the quiet neighborhood street that bordered the east side of our school, where the cafeteria, lunch area, and band room were. I turned my head slightly. I squinted through my glasses so I could see the street corner that Gregor was talking about.

And broke out into a sweat.

He was there. Sitting casually in his VW Bug. The peace sign like some kind of hippie beacon on the side of the car. When my eyes met his, DiCarlo lifted his chin as if to say, "Hey."

I suddenly felt a gob of grape jelly and bread glom up in my throat. I started choking and had to fish out my warm Gatorade bottle from my bag and take a swig to get it down. I tried to catch my breath.

"What do we do, Gregor?" Panic spread through my whole body, giving me this intense desire to start running.

"We could tell the noon aide lady," Gregor said, his voice shaky.

"That *what*? There's a guy sitting across the street in a car? He hasn't done anything but show up at my house and know my name! That's not a crime." My voice was rising to near-hysterical levels.

"You don't need to yell at me, Spencer." Gregor's tone was defensive. "You asked what we should do."

I sighed. "Okay, let's think about this." I glanced back at DiCarlo. Still there. Still looking at us.

"What if he knows where Ed is? Or Mel? Or

what if he can help us figure out *Pandora's Book*?" A little glimmer of hope ignited in my chest.

Gregor looked at me like I was nuts. "Or what if he wants to hack us up into forty million pieces and steal *Pandora's Book*?"

The glimmer of hope was snuffed out. "Yeah, there's that, too."

"But he probably wouldn't do that right here with all these other kids watching," Gregor added.

"Right," I said, nodding. "Good point."

"So maybe we should . . ."

A familiar raspy voice cut us off.

"Yo, Lemon." He was leaning up against the chain-link fence, casually, as if he were just taking a minute to catch his breath while out for an afternoon stroll. Except he wore a black trench coat, a fedora, and black dress pants that had dried mud caked near the cuffs. Same scuffed-up black-and-white shoes.

He didn't look happy.

"Look, I ain't got much time, kid," Frank DiCarlo said. "He's onto us, already."

I realized I was holding my breath. Gregor

looked like he might pee his pants any minute. I glanced at the other kids around us; they didn't seem to be paying much attention to Gregor or me or our unshaven visitor.

"What . . . what," I stammered, swallowing my terror. "What are you talking about?"

"The book, kid. He knows you got it. You need my help. Eddie told me to find you if this happened. He was worried this would happen." DiCarlo turned his head slightly, so I could see his eyes. They showed concern. "He was right, kid."

Eddie. Did he know where Ed was?

"Who are you?" I asked.

DiCarlo looked away and then leveled his gaze on me. This time, instead of concern, there was only calm resolve there. "A friend, Spencer."

His hand again went into his coat pocket. I didn't flinch. As he straightened up and backed a step away from the fence, he flicked a small card through one of its metal openings. It landed in the dirt.

"Page fifty-three, kid. You'll figure it out. Then, you call me, got it?"

Gregor and I watched, speechless, as he once again sauntered back to that brightly painted little car, squeezed himself in, and sped off, barely stopping at the corner before squealing around it on two wheels.

For the next thirty seconds, neither one of us moved. Then, Gregor reached over and picked up DiCarlo's card from the dirt. He handed it to me.

Silently, I read the card again. Frank DiCarlo, Broker, 909-555-4525.

"You gonna call him?" Gregor asked.

I shrugged, still looking at the card. Between you and me—I didn't know what I was going to do.

I shoved my half-eaten sandwich back into my bag and tossed the whole mess into the nearest trash can. Seconds later, I watched in disbelief as Gregor pushed his uneaten lunch back into his brown bag.

In nearly three years of our friendship, Gregor had eaten the same lunch every day: three orange slices, half a bologna sandwich with three dabs of mustard, three Oreo cookies, and a bag of Cheetos. He ate it in that order, every day—rain or shine, lunchroom or my living room, schooltime or summer. The only exception to the rule was the last Friday of every month, when his mom let him buy a slice of pizza from the cafeteria. Gregor lives for pizza.

In nearly three years, he'd never skipped lunch unless he had the stomach flu. Last year, his grandpa died and after the funeral, all his relatives gathered at his house for a buffet-style lunch. It was a serious feast: homemade macaroni and cheese, hot dogs and hamburgers, watermelon, chocolate chip cookies, chips and salsa, and cupcakes. I'd loaded up a plate and turned around to find Gregor, who had suddenly disappeared. I found him in the kitchen assembling three orange slices, half a bologna sandwich, three Oreos, and a bag of Cheetos.

Gregor tossed his lunch in the same trash can that I had. Then he grabbed his backpack, slipped it onto both shoulders, and looked at me expectantly.

"Come on, Spencer," he said. "It's time we figured out who he is."

Gregor spun around and started marching resolutely toward the library. Wordlessly, I grabbed my own backpack and followed.

CHAPTER 10
WE FIGURE OUT WHO
FRANK DiCARLO IS

Gregor and I sat side by side, our knees practically touching as we bent over the keyboard of one of the library's computers. I had *Pandora's Book* facedown on my lap, so no one could see the title of it. It just looked like a very old, very large encyclopedia. I was pretty sure no one would bug us. I mean, who uses encyclopedias anymore, anyway?

While the computer booted up, Gregor reached for *Pandora's Book*. "I think we should see who's on page fifty-three," he said.

I could only nod. It isn't often that Gregor takes charge like this. But when he does, picture James

Bond on a mission, only with tag-less shirts and constantly tapping fingers.

Together, we huddled over the book, turning pages. Page fifty-three had a large black-and-white photo of some guy I'd never seen before. He had a narrow face and dark, slicked-back hair, parted down the middle. Totally intense eyes.

"Eliot Ness," I read from the top of the page. "Wasn't he, like, an FBI agent or something?"

Gregor didn't answer me; he was already reading.

"Eliot Ness—born April 19, 1903, died May 16, 1957—was a law-enforcement agent, famous for trying to enforce Prohibition in Chicago, Illinois. Ness joined the US Treasury in 1927 and was given the challenge of taking down legendary gangster Al Capone. Ness assembled a team of men who were later nicknamed 'The Untouchables.' The efforts of Ness and his men seriously hindered Capone's operations. In a number of federal grand jury cases in 1931, Capone was eventually charged with several counts of tax evasion and thousands of violations of the Volstead Act. Capone was sentenced to eleven years in prison."

I looked at Ness's picture again. He didn't look anything like Frank DiCarlo. Too skinny.

"What do you think Eliot Ness has to do with Frank DiCarlo?" I asked.

Gregor looked thoughtful but didn't answer. Instead, he turned toward the computer and opened the Internet browser. Quickly, he typed something into the search box. Then, he clicked the mouse on the word *Images*.

Two dozen photographs, most of them black and white, filled the screen.

They were all of Frank DiCarlo. A clean-shaven, nicely dressed Frank DiCarlo.

I looked at Gregor. "What? How'd you do that?"

He pointed to the name he'd typed in the search box.

I swallowed and felt something like an ice cube slide across my chest.

I started to read the name there, but an angry voice from behind both of us did it for me.

"Al Capone," she said. "Frank DiCarlo is Al Capone, you idiots."

The girl standing behind us had short black hair that she tucked behind her ears. She stood with both hands on her hips, her eyes flashing, challenging. But there was something familiar about them, too. And though she had this I'll-gladly-kick-your-butt thing going on, she didn't look like some of the girls in my school who actually *did* kick people's butts. Those girls had hard eyes and chipped teeth and permanent scowls. This girl's teeth were perfectly straight and white. Her eyes were a soft, yellowish brown, like caramel topping.

I could see she was tall, a half inch taller than me actually, but not quite as tall as Gregor. Her face and arms were tan, like she spent a lot of time outside. She was in teal nylon shorts, a T-shirt that read GIRLS TRI HARDER, and running shoes—the expensive kind. Her legs—I couldn't help but notice—were long, lean, and muscular. Runner's legs.

"Who are you?" I repeated, noting Gregor's silence and hoping he wasn't about to leave James

Bond mode to go into a meltdown. If things got ugly with this chick, I might need him for backup. Or to at least run fast and get the librarian.

The girl continued to glare at both Gregor and me. Then she crossed her arms and lifted her chin defiantly.

"I'm Mel," she said.

My breath caught. She was real, then. Not just a creation of Ed's very active imagination. I tried to picture this slim girl running from a bull in Spain. Something about the look in her eye told me she might just be capable of it.

Mel kept glaring and looked prepared to put me in a headlock. Gregor was frozen in shock. Nobody seemed to want to make the first move. Somebody needed to do something.

I stood up, dropping *Pandora's Book* onto Gregor's lap, and assumed my own fighter stance. I was hoping I was somewhere between Jet Li and Nick Fury on the kick-butt scale.

"Who are you?" I asked, tightening my hands into fists. I'd never thrown a punch. Much less at a girl. But how hard could it be?

"I'm Mel," she said, rolling her eyes. "I already told you that."

"Yeah, I got that part," I said, growing angry. "But what are you doing here and how did you find us?"

"Not hard," she said, shrugging. "You go to school, right? So I found the school."

I felt my jaw tighten and pushed my glasses up my nose. She wasn't making this easy.

"How do you know about Frank DiCarlo?"

She snorted. "I could ask you the same question." Her eyes traveled over to Gregor, and she lifted her chin once in his direction. "He always act like that?"

Gregor was sitting on the edge of his chair ramrod straight, fingers tapping the cover of the book, eyes darting.

I moved so I was in front of him and felt my jaw harden. "He's fine," I said, with no small amount of edge to my voice.

Mel shrugged again, and her eyes softened. Just as quickly, though, the tough-girl attitude was back. "Maybe he's not your best candidate for a sidekick, then."

My fists clenched. "What do you want?"

Mel blinked, and her hand reached up to finger a pendant that hung from a thick chain around her neck. "Same thing you do. To find Ed."

I saw what flashed through her eyes. It was pain. I straightened out of my crouch.

"So you're not going to go all kung fu on me? And here I was worried." Her tone was mocking.

I felt my cheeks burn. And my anger return. "How do we know we can trust you? I mean, Ed said to find you, but . . ."

Mel's eyes narrowed. "Look, I know he gave you *Pandora's Book* and all, but that doesn't make you an expert in . . ."

"Wait!" I held up one hand. "You know about *Pandora's Book*?"

She scoffed. "Um, yeah. I know a heck of a lot more about it than you do. Why do you think he wanted you to find me?"

My brain was whirring, and I was starting to feel a tightness at the base of my skull. Could have been from testing this morning. Could have been because this was all so confusing. Either way, it wasn't a good sign.

I looked over at Gregor. He was still tapping, but his eyes looked more focused. He seemed to be following our conversation. That *was* a good sign; a meltdown here would really mess things up right now.

I turned and grabbed the book off Gregor's lap. Suddenly it felt important that I have it in my possession. Something about Mel made my stomach feel like I'd just ridden a roller coaster—like I needed to puke. I wasn't sure if I could put her in the "Good Guys" column yet.

Mel watched me with interest as I slid the book into my backpack and then slung everything up onto my back. She surprised me by offering up a tiny smile.

"Good," she said, nodding. "You need to be protecting it, Spencer. Always."

I didn't know which hit me more at that moment. The fact that she knew my name. Or that when she smiled, Mel was actually kind of pretty.

CHAPTER 11

WE SNEAK INTO ED'S ROOM

It was a good thing that the last test I had to take that afternoon was math and that it was basic algebra—stuff I was good at. I probably could've been half drugged and still gotten most of them right. Which is kinda what it felt like.

My brain was going haywire. All I could think about was that Frank DiCarlo was Al Capone, a notorious gangster who'd committed tons of nasty crimes in the 1920s. Who was now stalking us.

And when I wasn't thinking about Al Capone, I was focused on the fact that Mel was waiting for us at a small coffee shop. Thinking about her made me feel all roller-coastery. I wanted to go for a hard run or go hide out in my room or something. And I kept looking down at my shirt to see if I could puff out my chest and make it look bigger. Which was way weird. But it was also like I couldn't help myself.

Gregor and I had made plans to meet quickly after the final bell rang, hurry back to my house to drop off our stuff, and grab a snack, and then we were going to catch up with Mel and head over to the Everlasting Home for Seniors together. We didn't expect to find Ed there, but we were really hoping we could get into his room somehow. I don't know what we thought we would find in there, but maybe there'd be some kind of clue that might tell us what the heck was going on.

I also wanted to find out more from Mel. The bell had rung so quickly after she'd shown up that we hadn't had much time to talk. Had she met DiCarlo? Did she know where Ed might be? How did she know about the book?

By one thirty, I had Gregor balanced on the handlebars of my mountain bike and *Pandora's Book* shoved in a backpack. The day, thankfully, was cool with just some puffy white clouds clinging to the ridgeline of the low mountains that bordered our little town of Rio Valle. A perfect spring day in April. But still, warm, sticky crescents of sweat were rapidly forming around my neck and my armpits.

"Gregor," I gasped. "Do you think this is a good idea? Going to the nursing home and all?"

I wasn't convinced. My thighs weren't either.

Gregor, I gotta tell you, is a big kid. Not fat or anything like that—just tall and pretty muscular, like his mom. Me on the other hand—I'm short and wiry. Little legs that help me fly around the track when I want to. Little legs that were not doing a whole lotta good on this freakin' bike.

"Gregor, dude," I huffed, stopping for the eight-ieth time in fifteen minutes. "You gotta run. I can't,"—I gulped in air—"keep pedaling."

Gregor hopped off the handlebars. "Why do I gotta run? Why don't you run, Spencer?"

I took a much-needed swig from my water bot-tle. "Because you can't ride a bike for crap, dude." I wasn't being mean; it was the truth. By the time we got to the end of the block, he would have fallen at least eight times. No lie.

Gregor sighed and then took off down the street. I followed him, my legs rejoicing at the lighter load.

I watched my friend lope along, his long legs making the run look easy. He wasn't breathing heavily or even sweating much. But he was in the zone: his eyes trained on the sidewalk ahead, his arms pumping rhythmically, his feet lightly making contact with the ground before they pushed off into his next stride.

Gregor has perfect running form. A coach's dream. Except that he hates loud noises (every race starts with a loud gun blast), he doesn't like to be surrounded by a lot of people (which makes the mass start of the races a challenge), and he refuses to wear shorts (making him the only guy in the league to run with tights under his regulation uniform). And yet, he still wins just about every race.

With Gregor now running, we got to the coffee shop quickly. I slid my bike into one of the slots on the metal bike rack outside and offered Gregor my water bottle. You'd think I'd offered him warm pee by the look of disgust on his face. Another little

Gregor factoid for you: he won't drink from someone else's cup.

Stand Your Grounds Coffee House was pretty empty at this time of day except for a few college students studying for finals and one group of workout moms huddling over lattes. Mel was tucked behind a back corner table, typing frantically on a laptop, a really sweet pair of wireless Beats covering both ears. Whoever this chick was, she wasn't short on cash. Those things cost bucks. Big ones.

She saw us come in and hurried to jam everything into a checkered backpack that looked like it had just been pulled off the shelves of Tilly's that morning.

"So, you guys decided to show up," she said, tucking her hair behind both ears. "Wasn't sure you would." She didn't smile.

I watched her swiftly slip her iPhone into a side pocket of her backpack, but not before she checked it one last time. Who was she looking for? Ed? I didn't think he texted. DiCarlo? Someone else?

"We're here," I said decisively. "Let's go."

She grabbed her empty cup and effortlessly tossed

it toward the trash can that was at least twenty feet away. It dropped in neatly.

I wanted so badly not to be impressed. But the girl had mad aim.

Everlasting Home for Seniors was only a few blocks from the coffee shop. We decided to leave my bike where it was and get it on the way back. As the three of us walked in silence toward the nursing home, I tried to get up the courage to talk to Mel. Should I ask her what she knew? Demand she tell us about Frank DiCarlo? Trip her, grab her backpack, and take off with those killer Beats she had?

Instead, I just tried to keep up with her while admiring her long, lean legs. Finally, she turned to me.

"Did Ed tell you anything about the book?" she asked, looking hard at me.

I hesitated. He'd hardly told me anything. Whatever I knew about it, I was learning because A) all sorts of people were turning up asking about it, and B) Gregor and I had experimented by mistake. But I didn't really want Mel to know that last part.

I shrugged. "A little."

"He showed you how to work it though, right?" she asked, narrowing her eyes.

I shot a glance at Gregor. "Sure," I answered, trying to sound confident.

"So you know that when an important person dies, YOU have control over whether or not they make it into the book?"

I gulped. Ed had very much failed to mention that part. I had to hope that nobody really important died in the next few days. Until I could get the book back in Ed's hands, anyway.

I nodded. "Uh, yeah. I'm good," I said weakly.

"And you know that when you take a person out of the book, they can stay out as long as you want them to, but only YOU can put them back in?"

I sighed. Why hadn't Ed told me all of this? It would have been nice if this stupid book had come with an instruction sheet or something. Instead of just a white bookmark and a creepy stalker who was supposedly Al Capone.

"And you know that—"

"I got it, okay!" I said, glaring at her. "You're not

the only one who knows about the book. Plus, Ed gave it to me, not you, so he must have had a good reason for doing that, right?"

Mel looked like I'd slapped her. She quickened her step and didn't speak again the rest of our walk.

An older woman wearing a pink bathrobe sat on the bench in front of the EHS. But her chin was dropped low on her chest and as we got close, it was pretty clear she was sleeping. Or dead. Either way, she wasn't going to be bothered by our arrival.

"So, how are we going to do this?" I asked, grabbing my water bottle from my backpack and taking a big swig.

I was starting to feel prickles of apprehension in my stomach. This felt too much like we were breaking rules. I'm not good at breaking rules. I slid my glasses up my nose and looked nervously around like somebody was going to pop out of the bushes and scream, "Got you! We know you have the book! We know you lost Socrates!"

Gregor glanced toward the double glass doors that led into the lobby of the nursing home.

"I thought they knew you here, Spencer."

I nodded. "They do. But I usually come on Tuesdays and Thursdays. It's Wednesday."

I looked at Mel. Pointedly.

She threw up her hands. "Don't look at me, Agent Double-oh-seven! I've never set foot in this place. Ed forbade it."

She looked over at the front doors wistfully as if she actually wanted to spend time with all those glassy-eyed, shuffling, toothless people who called this place home.

Gregor's fingers started tapping. "Maybe this isn't a good idea, Spencer." He looked at his watch. "Almost two. Track practice is at three."

Track. I did a mental head-slap. I'd forgotten all about it. Gregor was going to have a fit if we didn't make it to track practice. The championships were in two weeks. Gregor hoped to break a five-forty-five mile time.

Maybe he was right. Being here wasn't a good idea. Maybe we should just go home and call the police or something. Or have my dad help us out.

But then I thought about what I'd have to tell him and how it involved a magical book, Socrates, and a guy who looked suspiciously like Al Capone. Who was going to believe us? I swallowed.

"We'll make it," I said with mock confidence. Inside, my heart was hammering. I glanced again at the front doors. "Come on, let's get this over with."

CHAPTER 12

WE RUN

I took the lead, trying to ignore the pounding of my heart. Mel and Gregor followed close on my heels.

My favorite receptionist, Sherri, was at the front desk. "Well, hey there, Spence," she said, standing up from behind her desk and flashing a set of perfectly straight, too-white teeth. A lot about Sherri could be described as "too." Too skinny. Too tan (for it to be real, anyway). Too perky. Somehow it all worked though. Sherri was gorgeous.

I smiled what I hoped was a winning smile. "Hey, Sherri."

She shot a quick grin at Mel. Then, her eyes drifted to Gregor who was staring not so subtly at a tattoo she had near her exposed collarbone that said

Angel. Somehow, I didn't think she meant the kind I saw in church.

"What's up, Spencer? What's going on?" Her eyes lost a little of their sparkle when she saw Gregor's ramrod-straight posture and his fingers tapping rhythmically on his thighs. Like most people when they first saw Gregor's slightly unfocused stare, his tapping fingers, his somehow out-of-whack body movements, she tried to cover up a grimace.

"These are my friends. This is Mel. And this is Gregor," I said. "I really wanted them to meet Ed."

I was praying that Sherri didn't know I'd called and already knew Ed was missing. I was also praying that she somehow didn't know Mel was his granddaughter.

Sherri's focus turned back to me and her lip-sticked lips curved down. "Oh, Spencer! You haven't heard?" She looked around furtively and leaned forward. "Ed's been missing since last night!"

I opened my eyes wide. "Missing? No way!" I looked over at Gregor. "Ed's missing, Gregor! Can you believe that?"

Gregor's eyebrows bent inward. "But, Spencer, we already ..."

Mel cut him off loudly. "Boy, that stinks," she said frowning, glaring at Gregor to shut up.

I turned back toward Sherri and slipped off my backpack. Quickly, I unzipped it and took out *Pandora's Book*. "He loaned this to me yesterday and I was hoping to give it back to him. Do you think I could maybe leave it in his room in case he, you know ... or when he ... um, gets back?"

Sherri nervously twirled a strand of her too-blond hair. "We're not really supposed to let anyone into his room, Spence. The police were here this morning, trying to take fingerprints and stuff, and questioning a few of the workers. I don't know."

"I understand," I said quietly and slid *Pandora's Book* back into my backpack. "I wouldn't want you to get in trouble or anything. It's just that, well, I know this book was important to him. You know, maybe I should put it back in his room in case ... I don't know ... maybe it could help the police or something?"

Sherri's brilliant blue eyes darted around the small

front room that served as a reception area. Other than one tiny, wrinkled guy who was balled into a corner of the couch, snoring softly, the area was deserted.

Sherri sighed. "Okay, go," she said quietly, already moving back behind her desk and picking up a nail file. "But be quick. And if anyone sees you, you're on your own."

I smiled a gigantic smile at her and hurried down the hall, figuring Mel and Gregor would follow.

"Great!" I said over my shoulder, my feet kicking up into a run. "No one will know we're here!"

Ed's door looked the same as it always did: no caution tape, just a cheap wooden nameplate that read, "Edward Elofson." I wondered if anyone ever really called him Edward.

I saw Mel reach up and finger the nameplate. For a second, I had to wonder how she was feeling. This was her grandpa. And though I still didn't understand their relationship, it had to suck that he was missing.

I thought the door might be locked, but it wasn't. I pushed inside quickly and let Gregor and Mel squeeze in with me. Then we latched the door closed behind us. For good measure, I slid the deadbolt into place. It wouldn't really keep anyone out since they probably all had keys, but it might buy us some time to hide, if we needed to.

Mel threw her backpack on Ed's bed and stood looking around, soaking everything in. Gregor stood just inside the door, his fingers tapping wildly against his legs.

"We shouldn't be here, Spencer," he muttered.

"How are we going to find out what's going on, if we don't start looking for clues?" I asked, setting my backpack on Ed's bed. "You wanna call Al Capone? Ask *him* what's going on?"

Gregor shook his head vehemently.

"He's not a bad guy," Mel said defensively. "Anymore, anyway."

"You know him?" I asked, feeling my eyebrows raise at least half an inch.

She shrugged and looked away. "Not really. But I've heard Ed talk about him. And I don't really understand all that's going on, but I'm pretty sure he's on our side."

I looked at her for a good long time. She was hiding something. A lot of somethings. It apparently ran in the family.

"All right then." I clapped my hands lightly. "Let's start looking around. For anything that might explain where Ed is."

The curtains in Ed's room were drawn and no lights were on. Some afternoon sun filtered through a crack between the curtains and under the door leading to the hallway. But it was dim and, well, creepy. And really hard for me to see. I flipped on the overhead light. Otherwise, I was pretty much useless.

Ed's bed, a narrow one on a metal frame like you might find in a hospital, was unmade. The top blanket was flung back, revealing grayish-white sheets. The mountain of pillows he liked behind his back to prop him up were messed up; one had even fallen off the bed and was on the floor. Like whoever got Ed out of bed didn't do it so gently.

Mel was rifling through his closet, a brave act since the stuff in there was likely full of mothballs, dust, and years of Ed-sweat. But he *was* her grandpa, so she could have at it.

Gregor wasn't really moving much, waiting to see what I was going to do.

I bent down and looked under the bed, but other than some dust bunnies—okay, a lot of dust bunnies—it was empty. His wheelchair was folded up in the corner, where he always kept it. The musty armchair that Ed claimed he'd had since the late 1950s sat where it always did.

Nothing looked out of place.

I walked over to his dresser and gently pulled open the top drawer. Underwear, neatly folded. I wrinkled my nose and closed the drawer quickly. The other two drawers were just as undisturbed.

I ran my hand through my hair. What exactly was I hoping to find here? A note that said *Dear Spencer, Let me tell you what's going on*? Not likely.

I sat down on his bed to think. It was so quiet. Not like when I came to visit Ed, who filled up this tiny room with his laughter and his stories. My chest tightened. What if something really bad had happened to him?

"I don't know, guys," I said, heaviness settling into my tired limbs. "Maybe we're off base here. Maybe this was a stupid idea."

Gregor had wandered over to the grandfather clock and was looking at it intently.

I stood up. "Come on, man," I said, grabbing my backpack. "Let's get Mel and . . ."

"Spencer," Gregor said softly. "Is this clock always like this?" His head tilted sideways, but I couldn't see what he was staring at.

I took a step toward him. "He got that clock from his grandfather," I said automatically, thinking back to two weeks ago when he'd told me the whole story of the clock and why it was so important to him. "His grandpa had been a clock maker and this had been the first . . ."

I stopped. Froze. The room was deathly still. *Too* still.

And now I knew why that was strange.

The clock was not ticking. The pendulum which usually swung back and forth in its case was motionless. It had always been ticking when I'd been here before.

I threw my backpack on the bed again and crossed the room to Gregor.

He pointed at the clock's large face. "Look."

The hands were stopped at precisely 1:34. Weird. Was that when he'd left or been taken? No, I was here that day from four o'clock to five and so was Ed. Gregor had called the nursing home at about six, and we learned he was missing. So why did the clock stop at 1:34?

Mel's head popped out of the closet.

"What's going on?" she asked no one in particular.

Slowly, Gregor reached up and unclasped the latch of the clock face. The glass door swung outward.

"Grandfather clocks were first invented in the seventeenth century," Gregor said, going into professor mode. "Supposedly by an English guy named William Clement . . ."

The jiggle of the door handle to Ed's room made

us all freeze. My heart started pounding. Gregor's fingers started tapping. His eyes widened, and I could see him begin to rock back and forth on his heels. Mel waved frantically at both of us, grabbed her own backpack off the bed, and motioned us into the closet.

My pulse pounding in my ears, I tiptoed toward the closet door with my backpack clasped to my chest. I could hear Gregor shuffling along close behind me. His breathing was way heavier than it had been when he was running over here. I had to keep him calm or we were in big trouble.

Two voices filtered through the door as the three of us slid into Ed's large walk-in closet. It was really dark in there and musty. The dust tickled my nose, but I quickly pinched my nostrils and held my breath.

I could barely make out what was being said outside.

"You think we're supposed to clean in there today?" It was a woman's voice. Not Sherri's. Not Nurse Margaret's.

"It's locked," the other woman said. "We probably

ought to ask somebody. Police were here earlier, you know. Doing all that *CSI* stuff."

"I heard Margaret tell the owner that they didn't find a thing. Not a thing! Can you believe it? He just disappeared into thin air!"

Their voices got fainter and I couldn't hear what they were saying anymore. I let out the breath I was holding, released my nose, and sneezed loudly.

"Jeez, Spencer," Mel said, throwing open the door. I didn't need to see her face to know that she was scowling. "And I thought Gregor was going to be the lousy snoop."

I felt my cheeks get warm. "Sorry," I mumbled as we tumbled out of the closet.

I turned back toward Gregor. "What were you saying about the clock again?" I asked, brushing cobwebs from my hair and tossing my backpack down again.

"What about the clock?" Mel asked, her head snapping up.

"Gregor thought it was weird that . . ."

She shoved past me so quickly I almost fell over. "Show me."

Gregor was still hovering near the door of the closet, looking like a deer about ready to bolt.

"Spencer." He tapped the face of his watch. "Two-thirty, Spencer. We'll be late."

Argh!!! Track practice.

If we left then, we could probably haul butt and make it just barely on time. But that meant leaving now and leaving Mel. And she seemed to be maybe the only one, besides Frank DiCarlo/Al Capone, who might know what was going on with *Pandora's Book* and with Ed. Plus, she was . . . something. Something that made me feel like I'd just drunk a whole two-liter bottle of Pepsi. And I liked that feeling.

I closed my eyes. How to explain this to Gregor?

Gregor stood up. "Coach P. says I can't miss practice, Spencer. Big race in two weeks." His fingers found his thighs and went to town.

I stared at him helplessly for a second. "Gregor, listen," I said calmly. "We do have a big race coming. But this is important, too. Ed's missing, Gregor." I glanced at Mel, not wanting to reveal too much yet. "I think we need to keep looking. Which means staying here right now."

"What's up with the clock, Gregor?" Mel asked again, insistently. Her eyes were roving over the face of it.

"Hang on a minute!" I said to her.

She reached up and tapped one of the hands with her finger. I saw her shake her head.

"Unbelievable," she muttered. "Freakin' unbelievable."

Gregor's eyes darted between Mel and me.

"But it's Wednesday, Spencer. Three o'clock on Wednesday means track practice."

I took a deep breath. "I know, man, but . . ."

Mel spun around, looking fierce and determined. "We could run." She rolled her shoulders a few times like the idea sounded really good to her. "Together. To your practice or whatever."

"Yes." Gregor walked toward the door. "Run to practice. Great idea."

Mel grabbed her backpack and moved to follow him.

"Hold on!" They both turned at the urgency in my voice. "We're just going to leave? What if there are more clues here? We don't even know who Mel really is and . . ."

Mel whipped around, her hair snapping around with her. "Look. I told you who I am. Ed's my grandpa. Great grandpa, actually. You can believe me or not. But you don't have a lot of options now, do you?" Her eyes dared me to interrupt her. "You don't know how *Pandora's Book* works. You don't know where Ed is. And you must be freaking out a little bit, or why else would you have come here to snoop around in his room with me?"

Her eyes bored into mine.

"Your friend wants to run. I want to run. We can't stay here. So, you got a better idea?"

I didn't. But I didn't like that Mel seemed to be holding all the cards.

I planted my feet. "We don't even know if we can trust you."

She sighed a loud, exasperating sigh. "You are one freakin' impossible per—"

She froze. Her body tensed, and she lifted one finger to her lips.

"Listen."

Click-click-click. Footsteps. Hurried ones. More than one set. One of them in what sounded like heeled boots.

"Sir!" That was Sherri. She sounded frantic. "You can't go in there! I told you that the police have, like, sealed it off or whatever. You can't . . ."

The other voice was deep. Harsh. "And I told you zhat I do not care vhat zee police haf done. Zhere's zomething in zhat room I need."

Thick German accent. Germans always sound kind of pissed off to me. This one sounded royally pissed off.

Suddenly, Mel grabbed me by the arm.

"Spencer. We've got to get out of here. *Now.*"

Mel closed her eyes and shook her head. When she opened them, her face was anxious.

"Snap, crackle, and pop! I knew he'd get here quickly. Just not this quickly." She looked at me, threw me my backpack, and pointed at the window.

"Go. Now. Out the window. We've got to get out of here before he sees you."

The steps outside were closer. Sherri's voice was loud and clear through the door.

"I'm calling security," she said, her voice shaking.

The man laughed—a derisive, nasty laugh. "Vonderful. Call zhem."

He was right outside the door. We had only seconds.

I spun toward the window. "Gregor! Let's go. Now's your chance to run, man!"

I pulled back the curtain and yanked the flimsy window up. Thank God Ed had a first-floor room. Just a few feet and we could jump to the ground.

I threw all my weight against the screen, which popped out easily. I could hear Mel right behind me. I looked over my shoulder.

Gregor wasn't moving.

My heart was in my throat. "Gregor! Please! We'll go to track practice, okay?" I pleaded with him.

His eyes were wide open. Wild. His hand still gripped the doorknob. I saw him glance back and forth—me to his hand to the door, me to hand to door.

"Gregor," Mel said in a calm, steady voice. "What's your best mile time?"

Gregor blinked. Then like a robot, he answered, "Five-fifty."

Mel smiled. "Show me."

For some reason, that did it. He released the doorknob and jogged to me. In one fluid move, he was over the windowsill and into the planter below.

The door handle jiggled violently from the outside. Whoever was out there wanted in. Badly.

"Sir!" Sherri was practically hysterical. "Please! Don't!"

Mel pushed away the curtains and jumped through the window. She landed neatly on two feet, like a cat.

I had one leg up and over the windowsill. I was gripping the straps of my backpack, ready to jump, when there was a deafening blast behind me. I felt the wall I was sitting on shudder. A glass pitcher on Ed's nightstand crashed to the floor. Startled, I fell forward, nearly toppling Mel.

"What was that?" I asked, scrambling to my feet and preparing to bolt across the yard.

"That was a guy you don't want to meet," she said, looking toward Gregor, who was a good ten yards ahead of us. "He just blew the door off its hinges. And if we're not careful, we're next."

Then Mel started running after Gregor with the most perfect form I'd ever seen on a girl.

CHAPTER 13

I LEARN WHO MY FRIENDS ARE
(AND WHO THEY AREN'T)

Mel was a runner. By the end of the block, she'd nearly caught Gregor who, despite not having his track shoes on, was hauling butt. I guess having a door explode behind you improves your mile time.

I was trailing along last—struggling with my heavy bouncing backpack and the jeans I was wearing. I wished I had my bike—I might have been able to keep up with the other two. We stopped at a corner to let a car go past, and I was grateful for the few seconds to catch my breath. I didn't like feeling that I was the one struggling.

Mel kept looking behind her. But I was too worried about Gregor to lose sight of him. Gregor was running with everything he had, tracing the route toward the school with single-minded focus. He looked neither right nor left, only straight ahead. I was afraid that in his quest to either beat Mel or get as far away from the chaos of Ed's room as possible, he was going to dart out into a street and get creamed by a bus or something. So I kept my eyes trained on him and watched at every cross street to make sure he was okay.

After about ten minutes, Mel slowed up enough to run along next to me. "We might have lost him. But you've got *Pandora's Book*, so we won't be safe for long."

We were running at a pace very close to what I would have run in a race. And yet Mel was able to breathe and talk like we were sitting across the lunch table from each other. I wanted to throw my backpack at her and yell, "You carry it!" But then she would have the book. And I still didn't know if she was friend or foe yet.

While we ran, a million questions formed in my head. Who was after us? That was the first and most pressing one. But I also wanted to know how Mel knew all this. What did she know about *Pandora's*

Book? And why was she so willing to take off with us? Weren't her parents wondering where she was? This was all just so strange. But if she hadn't been in the room with us, who knows what would have happened. It might not have been the door splintering into tiny pieces . . . but Gregor and me.

It wasn't until we reached the front driveway of our school that Gregor slowed down. He waited for us, panting, before he turned automatically toward the gym and the locker rooms.

Campus was nearly deserted, since school had ended early. Even though it had been an early out, Coach P. always scheduled practice for three o'clock, because he taught at the high school, and they didn't get out as early as we did. I didn't know exactly what time it was—Gregor was the guy with the watch— but I figured we were probably a few minutes late. Coach P. would not be happy.

Gregor pushed right into the boys' locker room to change into his track clothes and shoes. I stopped and tried to catch my breath. Mel kept looking around, her eyes stopping for a few seconds in every direction to see if he—whoever *he* was—had followed us. But she didn't seem to be struggling after that mad dash we'd just made. And I hated her for it.

"So. See you." I started to walk away.

"Wait!" The intensity of Mel's voice stopped me cold. I turned to face her. "Be careful, okay? You're probably safe in a place like this with lots of people around." She looked up and down the hallway. One teacher was locking up her room. The custodian was wheeling his large cart in the other direction. "But when you leave here later . . ."

I didn't like the *probably*. Or the way her words trailed off.

"Where will you go?" I asked. I didn't trust her as far as I could throw her. But maybe it was better to know where she was. Keep your friends close and your enemies closer, right? Plus, she was probably in just as much danger as we were. Either way, leaving her alone didn't seem like such a great idea.

She shrugged. "Maybe I'll find a place off to the side and watch you guys run." There was something sad in her eyes.

"Do you run track?" I asked, unable to help myself. I was way too curious about her. "At your school?"

Mel got a faraway look.

"I wish." She snorted. "Crestview Prep isn't exactly big on athletics. We're more of an artsy school." She said *artsy* like it was a disease.

I'd heard of Crestview. It was a super-expensive junior high a few miles west of here. I was pretty sure that celebrities' kids went there.

"Don't you have class today?"

She shrugged. "I had my nanny call me in sick. She owed me one because I caught her trying on my mom's French perfume last week and promised not to tell. Anyway, it's not like anyone really cares what I do."

I stared at her. She had to be about my age. Maybe even a little younger. How could no one care about where she was? I shook my head. She was full of as many mysteries as her grandfather. But I didn't have time to figure them out now.

"Okay, then," I said and started to lean on the locker room door to open it. "I guess I'll see you around."

She laid her hand on my arm. I jumped. I was hot

and sweaty from running, but her fingers still felt like a lit match on my skin.

"Spencer," she said, her warm brown eyes growing serious. "We need to talk about some things. After practice. There's stuff you have to know."

What she was saying was important, but I could only concentrate on the feel of her hand on my arm. When she pulled it away, my body felt way colder.

Mel walked slowly in the opposite direction, toward the track.

"Mel!"

I slipped my arms out of the backpack. Held it out to her. I didn't know why I was doing it, but it was like some inner voice wanted me to.

"Maybe you should watch over this. You know, while I run?"

Her lips twitched upward into something like a grin, but it vanished quickly. Nodding, she reached out for my backpack. "Yeah." She turned away.

With a shaky sigh, I hurried into the locker room, knowing I was going to be on Coach P.'s list for being late.

• • •

"Lemon! You got an extra eight hundred. Now, move!"

My legs were already tapped from the mad dash we'd made from the nursing home to get here. But when Coach Petrovinski—see why we call him Coach P.?—said, "move," you moved.

Gregor must have just slid onto the track in time for warm-ups, because while I ran an additional two laps of the track, he was with the rest of the team, stretching and going through drills. He gave me a nervous, apologetic glance, but quickly dug into the drills. Gregor takes running very seriously. For the next hour, he would put every cell of his body into doing what Coach said and making sure he was the fastest guy out there. Chances were good that he would cross the line first every time.

On my last lap, I noticed Mel had found a spot against the back fence. She'd propped my backpack next to her and was leaning against her own, sitting with legs stretched wide, back up against the fence, her hair swirling into her face with every breeze. As I rounded the corner of the track nearest to her, she waved her hand in subtle acknowledgement. I tried to slide my eyes away and ignore her but found myself glancing her way, almost against my will. Though I'd been feeling sluggish, seeing Mel sent a current of energy down my spine and into my legs. I finished the lap with solid, measured strides.

Still, by the time we'd run through our workout for the day—four 400 pushes, each followed by an 800 recovery—I was cooked. My calves were tight and burning. My chest was heaving. And my head ached. In the dim light of the locker room, it got harder for me to see. I had to strain to make out more than just big shapes.

Gregor sat down next to me as I pulled my street clothes from my locker and wadded them in a ball to shove in my backpack once I'd found Mel. I wished I'd thought to bring more than one water bottle in my backpack, since that one was long since empty. My tongue felt swollen. Even my ears were ringing a little bit from the dehydration.

"My four hundreds were all under one minute and ten seconds," Gregor said, chugging water from his own water bottle. I didn't know where he got the bottle since he didn't have one earlier. Maybe it was in his locker or something. I watched him with envy but knew better than to ask him for a drink.

"That's great." My voice held little enthusiasm. I was just too tired.

"You were slow today."

I sighed. Gregor doesn't always understand subtlety or politeness. He simply states what he thinks are obvious facts.

"Yeah, man," I said, slamming my locker closed. "Too much running on the way to practice."

"But we outran the bad guy, didn't we?" I could feel him smile next to me.

Gregor and I decided to stay in our running clothes—me in my shorts and T-shirt, him in his long tights and shirt with the tag cut out—and shower later, when we got home. As Gregor was locking up his PE locker, I turned to him. "You going home?"

Sometimes, on Wednesdays, his Dad got off early and picked him up from practice. Other times, he came home with me.

Gregor shook his head. "My dad has a meeting. He said to go home with you."

I looked at him thoughtfully. "I need to talk to Mel. She has *Pandora's Book*. I've got to find out what she knows. You okay with that?"

For a minute, he didn't say anything. He stared at his shoes. "I think you should listen to Mel," he said quietly.

I was shocked. Gregor generally didn't like new people. He takes forever to warm up to strangers. Every year—even though his mom pulls strings to make sure he and I are in the same classes—it's painful trying to get him to go to school until about November, when he will finally decide that he likes his teachers.

Gregor looked up at me and then back at the ground. He kicked the toe of his shoe lightly against the bottom locker.

"Spencer," he said, and his voice was measured, like he was trying hard to make his words sound important. "*Pandora's Book* is . . . I mean, the people in that book, they're all really important people, you know?

From history. Together, they did a lot of great things. So I think it's important that you keep it safe, okay? Like protect it." He looked up at me, found my eyes, and held them. Steadily. "And I want to help you." His hands rested calmly at his sides. His breathing was regular. I could tell that this was really important to him. "I want to try to help, okay?"

I nodded.

There was a lot he wasn't saying but kind of was, if that makes any sense. We both knew that stressful situations were even more stressful for him. That he would have to work hard to stay in control of his emotions and his body.

But it didn't surprise me. What he was offering.

It didn't surprise me because Gregor's whole life has been one challenge after another. And he never backs down. He might freak out now and then, but he plows through in his own James Bond way.

It didn't surprise me because Gregor loves history more than anyone in the world. To him, the people in *Pandora's Book* were worth protecting. Worth fighting for.

But mostly—it didn't surprise me because Gregor was my friend. He would have jumped through a wall of fire for me. In fact, I was pretty sure that part of the reason he stayed by the door back in Ed's bedroom—when he knew that whoever was on the other side was Number One Bad Dude—was because staying there meant he was between me and that guy. Whatever nastiness was about to happen, he would take it on first.

I swallowed the lump that was pushing its way into my throat. "Okay," I said, pulling in a deep breath. "Let's go find Mel."

We walked out into the bright California sunshine a few moments later. The school was mostly deserted. Just a few stray kids, like us, having wrapped up practice or some other after-school activity. And a handful of tired teachers scrambling to finish grading or whatever else teachers did after school. But the normally crowded hallways were silent.

We walked slowly back toward the track, figuring we'd find Mel still sitting up against the fence or maybe wandering toward the locker rooms to meet us. We didn't talk. I think the events of the day were finally catching up with both of us. We were tired, but more than that, we were a little anxious about what we might find out from Mel. What might come next.

When we got back out to the track, I stopped and shielded my eyes from the sun with my hand. Sure, my eyes were exhausted and my vision pretty blurry. But I didn't see anyone up against the fence. No one walked toward us from the field. We were the only two people out there.

"Do you see her?" I asked quietly, turning in a circle, hoping to find her tall, lanky shape walking toward us. Nothing.

Gregor shook his head. "Did she say where she'd meet us?"

I shook my head. "She just said she wanted to talk to me after practice. That's it. But she was sitting over there the whole time." I pointed toward the fence.

Gregor squinted in that direction. "She's not there now."

Something was rising up in my chest. Like a tidal wave or a swarm of bumblebees. Or my peanut butter sandwich from lunch.

"Where is she?" I muttered, my voice shaky.

I started to walk back toward the locker rooms. "Maybe she went to the bathroom or something, right? I mean, could we have missed her?"

Gregor said nothing, but we both quickened our pace.

The hallway in front of the locker rooms was deserted. No Mel.

"Where would she go?" I asked, though I knew Gregor had no more answers than I had.

My body was starting to shiver a little. I couldn't avoid acknowledging the thought that was worming its way up into my brain.

"Gregor." I turned to him. "She has the book. She stole it, Gregor. If she's gone, so is *Pandora's Book*."

CHAPTER 14
WE TEAM UP WITH A PRESIDENT
(WELL, A DEAD ONE)

Gregor and I didn't say much on the walk to my house. I don't live far from the school—it takes only about five minutes walking—and I think we were both hoping that Mel would somehow pop out from behind a bush or something and say that she was sorry, she got lost, all just a misunderstanding.

I probably don't have to tell you this, but that didn't happen.

It was about four thirty by the time we made it back to my house. I flopped down on my bunk bed, totally wiped out. I was kicking myself a hundred times over for trusting Mel. How could I have been so stupid?

"Maybe it's not what it seems," Gregor said as he pulled my desk chair out to sit down. "Maybe she needed to do something with it. Maybe she knows where Ed is, and she took it to him. Maybe she's putting it in a safe place, and then she'll come find you."

I looked at him over the top of my glasses. He was all blurry and indistinct. Kind of like my life right now.

"Yeah, and maybe the guy who shot the door off its hinges back at the hospital was really coming to tell us we'd won the lottery."

I closed my eyes and let the rumbling of my stomach and the pounding of my head overtake me.

"No, I don't think he was doing that, Spencer," Gregor said seriously. "We're too young to win the lottery anyway." (FYI: Gregor doesn't get sarcasm.)

I'd done so much wrong in the past twenty-four hours. That's all it had been: just twenty-four hours. And in that time I'd taken a powerful book that I knew nothing about and hadn't bothered to get the instruction manual for. I'd let my overanxious friend give it a try and wound up with Socrates in my bedroom, who we'd then lost and who was now wandering around the Los Angeles area with the other freaks, homeless guys, and drug addicts. I'd somehow gotten on the radar screen of Frank DiCarlo/Al Capone, who was stalking me—but who, never fear, Mel said was *probably* on our side. And I'd handed over *Pandora's Book* to a complete stranger, simply because she had awesome legs.

Dear God, I prayed suddenly, *can you help me out a little? Forgive me for being so completely and utterly stupid.*

"Spencer," Gregor said softly. "I liked her, too. I would have given her *Pandora's Book*, too."

Great. That meant we were both idiots.

I forced my eyes open and hauled myself up to a sitting position.

"So what do we do now?" I asked, feeling helpless. "Just wait for somebody to turn up? Maybe the German guy from the nursing home? Maybe Ed? Maybe Socrates? DiCarlo? Mel? Maybe a genie in a bottle who can grant us a wish and make this whole mess go away?"

"There are no genies in a bott—" Gregor started to say.

"I know!" I yelled, frustrated.

Gregor was quiet. He wouldn't look at me.

After a long minute, he said quietly, "You remember the first cross-country meet we ran in sixth grade?"

It would be a hard one to forget. We were competing against the two largest schools in our league. They each had about one hundred runners. Which meant that the starting line was packed. Which meant that Gregor was nearing a complete meltdown.

We were standing in that giant pack of kids, and Gregor was having a really hard time. He wanted to bolt—and not toward the finish line. He was ready to quit. Go home. Never run again. I was doing everything in my power to keep him holding on to sanity long enough for the gun to go off. Then I knew he would fly, and the rest of us would have a hard time just keeping up.

"I can't run with all these people." He repeated this over and over, like a mantra. His eyes kept darting everywhere; his body was shaking. His hands were up, and he was tapping his fingers frantically against his chest.

"You're not going to run *with* them," I remembered saying. "You're going to run *ahead* of them."

We were up on the line—Coach having made sure that the two of us were in good positions to get out in front and stay there.

"Don't look back at them," I'd said. And then I risked having him freak by physically turning his body so it faced the course. "Focus on what is in front of you. And on what you have to do. You set the pace, okay? Make them keep it. You're Pheidippides, remember?"

He had half smiled then. "And you're Koroibos."

Roughly thirty seconds later, the gun went off, Gregor went flying, and it was the first of many races in which Gregor did indeed set the pace and make the rest of us keep up.

"Yeah, I remember that day," I said to him now. "You kicked everybody's butt, dude."

Gregor smiled. "Yeah, but if you hadn't said what you said at the start line, I never would have raced.

Spencer, I think about that before every single race. Don't look back. Focus on what's ahead. Set the pace and make them keep up with us."

I chuckled. "Pretty good advice, if I do say so myself."

"So do it, Spencer."

"What?" I said.

"Take your own advice." Gregor shook his head like he was frustrated that I wasn't getting this. "You can't change what's done. So quit looking back. Focus on what's ahead. And don't wait for them to come to you. You set the pace."

"But I don't know where they are, Gregor. That's the whole problem!" I slammed my fist down on the bed.

He pulled a card from his pocket. "Maybe you don't know where Mel is. Or Ed. But one guy keeps telling you to call him. Maybe you should."

I took the card from his hand. Frank DiCarlo. Al Capone. But was he one of the good guys or the bad guys? There was really only one way to find out.

"My cell phone was in my backpack with *Pandora's Book*," I said. "You got yours?"

"Yeah, but you know my mom checks it all the time. You better use the house phone," Gregor said.

We had a cordless, but since my mom, dad, and I all had cell phones, only Molly and telemarketers ever used it. I ran next door to Molly's room—wondering not for the first time how a sane person could stand to live in all that pink—and found the phone where I knew it would be: buried under a mound of dance leotards on her princess bed. *Blech.*

Gregor was pulling out my laptop when I walked back into my bedroom and flung the door closed behind me. My mom wasn't back from her yoga class yet, Molly was at dance class, and my dad wouldn't be home until sundown, but I didn't want anyone walking in on this conversation.

"What are you going to look up?" I asked Gregor while I started punching in the numbers that I read off DiCarlo's card.

"Just checking something out," he said cryptically. I shrugged. A web-surfing Gregor was a subdued Gregor. Worked for me.

I had just hit the Call button on the phone when

something occurred to me. I quickly disconnected the call. Instead, I punched in the number to my own cell phone. It was a long shot but worth a try. I'd set the phone on vibrate, I was pretty sure. Maybe Mel would hear it and pick up.

Instead, after the third ring, a deep male voice barked, "Who is zhis?" German accent.

For a second, I couldn't move. Breathing wasn't working out too well, either. I knew that voice. It was the same one that had been out in the hallway at the nursing home.

A picture of Mel leaning against the fence scurried through my brain. I saw her wave at me and smile. My heart dropped into my stomach. She hadn't taken off. She'd simply been taken.

I hung up.

"Gregor." My voice was barely above a whisper, and I was shaking. "He has Mel. The guy. The guy from the nursing home. Has Mel. And *Pandora's Book*."

My words were like rushing water, plunging out of my lips and over a very steep cliff. Falling into an abyss.

Gregor looked up, startled. "What?" His fingers froze above the keyboard.

"The guy. With the German accent. Has Mel. He just answered my phone."

I saw Gregor wince and his eyes start to dart. He pulled one hand back to his chest to tap. Then, he closed his eyes. Took a deep, deep breath. Stilled his hand. And looked straight back at me.

"So how do we find her?" he said.

I leaned over him and pointed to the laptop screen. "That app on my phone. Remember the one I downloaded that will track it if I lose it? Hurry."

For a second, Gregor just looked confused. Then understanding clicked in, and he couldn't type fast enough.

A home screen popped up for the site.

"My email address. XCboy01@ ..." Gregor typed like a maniac. He knew the rest.

"Password?" he asked.

"Pheidippides."

I didn't even have to tell Gregor how to spell it. When I'd gotten my phone, I'd immediately signed up for an app that allowed you to track your phone if you lost it or someone stole it. I'd never had to use it. Until today. We'd see if it really worked.

For a second, a box popped up that said, "Spencer's phone locating." There was a light blue and gray map of the world behind it. Gregor and I both held our breath.

Then magically, a new screen appeared. It was a map with labeled streets and parks. In the center of the map was a bright blue dot with a circle around it. A dialogue box with an arrow pointed to the dot. It said, "Spencer's phone."

Gregor covered his mouth and froze. I felt like I'd taken a sucker punch to the gut.

For a long minute, we couldn't speak. We could only stare at the location on the map.

"Well, now we know where she is," I said quietly.

Gregor was still stiff and unmoving. I could see the fear threatening to take over his body. And I could see him fighting it. But he was losing. He was shutting down.   .

"You don't have to do this," I said. "I'll call Frank

DiCarlo. He can go. Or the police maybe. This would be kidnapping, right?"

My hands were shaking. I pushed my glasses up my nose. I had a horrible image of Mel, her long beautiful legs tied together with scratchy lengths of rope, cutting into her skin. A rag stuffed in her mouth. But she'd be fighting him. Somehow I knew she would be.

And I smiled. If she could fight, I could, too.

Gregor still hadn't moved. I was starting to get really nervous. For him. For me. For Mel.

I closed my laptop. I knew the address. Didn't need to write it down.

"You stay here, okay?" I said to Gregor as I stood up.

"How did he know?"

I barely heard him, he was talking so softly.

I swallowed and fought the tears that wanted to come.

"I don't know," I said.

"Athena," he murmured.

Oh, dear God. If something happened to that dog . . .

In the summer before fifth grade, Gregor had

wanted a dog. Desperately. He was fixated on it. And believe me, nobody can fixate on something like Gregor. He brought it up constantly. He begged. He whined. He researched how pets sometimes helped kids with autism focus. Mrs. Chandramouli didn't relent.

"Dogs are big, troublesome beasts who chew on furniture and leave big poops in my yard," she said emphatically in her thick accent.

I should tell you that although Gregor's dad is Indian and a stocky guy who is only about five feet tall, his mom is Swedish. She towers over Gregor's dad, has nearly translucent skin, hair the color of straw, and the body of a runner. It's this weird mix of Indian and Swedish genes that gives Gregor his dark skin, dark hair, and blue eyes.

As Mrs. Chandramouli swung her head from side to side, the thick blond-white braid that snaked down her back swung with her. "No, Gregor. Absolutely not."

So anyway, one day that summer, Gregor and I were hanging outside one of the shops that lines the single block that's downtown Rio Valle. Mrs. Chandramouli was in the bookstore. Gregor and I were waiting on a bench, slurping up ice cream cones. There was a pet store next door, and Gregor was going on and on about his perfect dog.

"Probably a Labrador, though a golden retriever would be good, too. I would train her to lie by my feet and get me things when I wanted them. Definitely a girl dog since boys are more aggressive and they pee on everything."

He was talking a mile a minute, pausing only to take a lick of his ice cream. I was pretty much ignoring him, thinking about going for a swim later that day and wondering if my prescription goggles might be ready for pickup from the doctor's office.

Just then a girl, maybe high-school age, started walking toward us. She held a leash, and attached to the end of it was a friendly looking golden retriever. Gregor stopped talking, dropped his ice cream on the bench next to him, and like a magnet to a refrigerator, started making his way toward that dog.

While I picked up what remained of his cone and

swiped at the icky mess on the bench with a napkin, Gregor dropped to his knees and went gaga over that big, hairy dog.

Keep in mind: if I slapped him high five, Gregor went "Ew!" and ran off to scour his hands in a gallon of antibacterial soap. But that dog was licking Gregor's face like *he* was the ice cream cone, and Gregor didn't even flinch.

"What's his name?" Gregor asked the girl.

"Dracula," she answered, seeming bored. She started picking at her fingernails, while Gregor cooed at the dog.

"Oh, Dracula," he said, nuzzling its neck. "Isn't that the best name for you, huh, boy?"

I glanced over my shoulder and through the front window of the bookstore, saw Mrs. Chandramouli grabbing her bag from the counter and shoving her purse back up her arm.

Then two things happened simultaneously. A fire engine that had been coming slowly down Main Street suddenly turned on its siren, scaring the pee out of everyone nearby. But whereas most of us just jumped and covered our ears, Gregor froze and went wide-eyed. At the same moment, three rowdy high-school boys came barreling down the sidewalk on their skateboards (ignoring the posted signs, by the way), narrowly missing Gregor, me, and the chick with the dog.

It was enough. Gregor lost it.

He curled into a ball and sank toward the sidewalk. He rocked on his heels so that his butt barely hit the ground. His arms encircled his knees, and he began moaning, doing that low-pitched hum he always does when he "melts."

The high-school girl backed away, her eyes wide and terrified, not wanting to stay but not wanting to leave him like that.

I ran over and knelt beside him.

"Gregor? Come on, man. It's cool. The siren's gone, dude."

Gregor's eyelids were half-closed, and his fingers tapped against his wrist on the opposite hand. I could just make out some of the words he hummed. "Zeus, god of thunder. Athena, goddess of wisdom.

Ares, god of war." On and on, he chanted the names of the Greek gods under his breath.

Gregor's mom came out of the store and rushed over. "What happened?" she said to me, dropping her bag of books on the sidewalk and squatting. "What set him off?"

"Fire engine," I said simply. Mrs. Chandramouli nodded.

I glanced up at the girl holding the leash of the dog. She looked scared to death, like she was about to be blamed for this mess. Her dog, meanwhile, had started sniffing at Gregor, nudging him with his wet nose.

Slowly, Gregor's rocking stopped. His shoulders dropped, and one hand released the other. He unfurled from his tight ball and cupped a hand under Dracula's muzzle. His other hand began stroking the dog just above the eyes. Dracula licked Gregor's face. Gregor smiled.

Mrs. Chandramouli gaped. She'd never seen Gregor come out of one of his meltdowns so easily. Neither had I.

"You know this dog, Gregor?" she asked.

Gregor didn't speak. He was too caught up in rubbing the dog—this kid who rarely touched anyone or anything. Quickly, Dracula rolled over and exposed his belly.

Mrs. Chandramouli glanced at me. Glanced at Gregor and Dracula. Glanced up at the pet store. Understanding seemed to cross her face.

Gregor got a new dog the following week. From the shelter, not the pet store since Mrs. Chandramouli refused to have a puppy. It was a golden retriever and Labrador mix. A sweet well-trained female that he named Athena. That he doted on, slobbered over, and had more physical contact with than any human.

If something had happened to Athena . . . if anyone had hurt Athena . . . I couldn't imagine what it would do to Gregor. I swallowed.

"She's fine," I said to him. But I didn't know that. The German guy was definitely high up in the "bad guy" category. I could only hope that he liked dogs.

Gregor stood up so abruptly that my desk chair fell

backward and hit the floor with a *thunk*. "I'm coming," he said. "It's my house. Athena's there. I'm coming."

I looked at him for a long moment. He probably shouldn't come. Gregor doesn't do well under pressure. No disrespect to him or anything. He just doesn't.

But a selfish and a really scared part of me didn't want to do this alone. Even a shaking, tapping Gregor would be better than no one. I closed my eyes. How had we gotten ourselves into this mess?

There was a knock at my front door.

My eyes popped open. Gregor was stock-still.

"Your dad?" I whispered, though I wasn't sure why I bothered to be quiet.

Gregor looked at his watch. Shook his head. "Too early," he mouthed.

Which meant it was a delivery guy. A door-to-door salesman. Frank DiCarlo. Or . . . I couldn't even imagine. The possibilities were endless. And included dead people.

I sucked in a breath.

"Guess we better go see who it is," I said with more confidence than I felt.

The knocking got more insistent as we made our way down the hall.

I peeked out the front curtains, but there was no car parked on the street in front of my house. And I couldn't see the front porch to know who was there.

Whoever it was knocked again. Harder. And called out, "Spencer? Spencer Lemon?"

Lemon. Like the sour yellow fruit. I rolled my eyes.

The voice was deep but clipped and maybe what I would call refined. Like somebody really rich and snooty. Not dangerous. I glanced one last time at Gregor, who had a don't-look-at-me expression. So, I sucked in a breath and threw open the front door.

The man looked me up and down over his tiny, round spectacles. He was a large man—not fat, but broad and muscular like someone who worked out. He seemed tall, even though he wasn't even six feet probably. He wore a funny-looking leather hat with one brim tucked up close to his head and had a dark-blue kerchief tied around his neck. Snug across his ample chest was a faded brown uniform with large brass buttons down the front. A wide leather belt held a long-handled knife sheathed in brass. On his hands were wide-cuffed gloves that came nearly up to his elbows. Scuffed boots. A bushy auburn mustache. And he looked familiar.

"You ready, young man?" the guy asked gruffly.

I glanced back at Gregor, who was wide-eyed but not tapping.

"Teddy Roosevelt?" he breathed.

The man raised an eyebrow. "Most folks call me Mr. President, but on account that we're headed into what may prove to be a skirmish, you two young fellows can call me Colonel Roosevelt."

I gaped at the man on my porch.

Down at his side, he gripped a long brown rifle—though I'm not a gun expert, I'd have said it was maybe a Winchester. The kind you might have gone hunting with. If you'd lived during the Civil War. It was *old*. But seemed like it could kick some serious butt if it needed to.

Which—given the German guy's actions of the last few hours—it just might need to.

Gregor launched into his Wikipedia mode.

"Theodore Roosevelt. Our twenty-sixth President. A colonel in the Spanish-American War who gathered volunteers to form the cavalry known as the Rough Riders. After his presidency, he led hunting expeditions in Africa and South America. A big supporter of the Boy Scouts of America."

"Well done, my boy," Roosevelt crowed, beaming. "A rightly good summary of my life."

I swallowed and pushed my glasses up my nose. "How did you know to come here?"

Roosevelt grinned broadly. "A young lady sent me. Said you two might need some assistance." He raised his rifle up with both hands and held it across his chest. "Now, we goin' by foot or by horse?"

CHAPTER 15

WE SAVE MEL . . . SORTA

Gregor doesn't live all that far from me. Which is a good thing because he and I were pretty close to hyperventilating on the walk to his house.

Roosevelt may have had a gun and some years of experience with the Rough Riders in the Spanish American War. But I'd gone toe-to-toe with Anthony "The Gut" Gutterson only once in my life—when he'd called Gregor a freak—and I'd come out of that with a royal headache after he'd dumped me upside down off the jungle gym.

Gregor and I had no real weapons—though we had grabbed an old backpack (since Evil German

Guy had my school one) and jammed it full of stuff we hoped might work if worst came to worst: an airsoft gun, an old slingshot that my dad had made for me years ago, a small pocketknife, and a bottle of pepper spray that my mom took when she went hiking. Beyond that, we had no fighting experience, no killer instincts, and no clue about what we were up against.

Roosevelt didn't seem at all concerned, though. He marched quietly along next to us, whistling a little, using the rifle as a cane now and then to tap the sidewalk. We could have been walking to the ice cream shop for all the concern he was showing. In fact, if I'd have sized up his mood, I would have said he was kind of excited about the whole thing.

Gregor was quiet, too, but it was a different quiet from Roosevelt's. His steps were small and measured. He was muttering under his breath, and though I couldn't hear him, I would have bet my entire college savings that he was reciting either Greek gods or important dates in history. His hands hung at his sides and his fingers tapped lightly but insistently on his thighs.

"Why did he go to my house, Spencer?" Gregor asked very softly when we were only a few houses away.

"I don't know, G.," I answered.

I didn't even know who "he" was. Just that he was German. And a really bad dude.

"If he has Mel and Mel has *Pandora's Book*," Gregor said, "why does he need us to come at all? Why not just take the book and go? He has what he wants, right?"

I shrugged. But it was that last part that made me extremely nervous. I'd just assumed it was *Pandora's Book* that this guy was after. Maybe it was something more. Maybe he needed me, too. That was the part that had me ready to pee my pants.

Colonel Roosevelt, Gregor, and I stopped on the corner to cross the street.

Roosevelt turned to us. "Can I assume you two lads know who our adversary is?"

"Actually, sir," I said, clearing my voice, "we don't. All we know is that the guy is German, he's mean, and he has a friend of ours. Well, kind of a friend, I guess. Her name is Mel." I could feel warmth creep into my cheeks.

"Mel is the young lady who sent me, I presume?" Roosevelt asked, looking down at us through his spectacles.

"I think so, sir," I said, nodding. "Did she, uh, say anything? Anything about what was going on? Why she was being taken?"

Roosevelt looked thoughtful for a moment and then reached into the brown bag he had slung on his hip.

"Pardon my absentmindedness, dear boy, but your friend said to give this to you as soon as I located you. I'm dismayed to say that I got so excited about the prospect of a skirmish with an outlaw that I completely forgot to pass it along. I do hope it was not imperative."

Gregor and I both gasped at the same time. Roosevelt was holding *Pandora's Book*.

Carefully, I took it from him. For a second, I just held it and felt its heaviness in my hands.

"He doesn't have it," Gregor said. "The German guy doesn't have it."

Relief poured through me. "No," I said, smiling. "He doesn't."

"Which is good, right, Spencer?" Gregor asked, his fingers tapping against his legs. "He can't do anything without this book, right? And he won't hurt Athena?"

I needed Gregor to stop talking for a second so I could think about this. I tried to look at things from the perspective of an extremely evil guy who was not above shooting at children or kidnapping a young girl to get what he wanted. Would he hurt a dog? Possibly. Could I tell Gregor that? No way.

Evil German Guy had Mel (we thought). And he was at Gregor's house. And at one point, he must have thought Mel had *Pandora's Book*, which was why he kidnapped her. But she sent *Pandora's Book* with Colonel Roosevelt. So what would Evil German Guy do next?

I didn't know. But I was pretty sure about one thing. When he found out that Mel *didn't* have

Pandora's Book, he was going to be one royally ticked-off Evil Dude. There was really no telling what he might do to her.

I tucked the book under my armpit and broke out into a jog. Roosevelt and Gregor trotted to catch up to me. We were only a few houses away from Gregor's. We could be there in minutes.

"What's wrong, Spencer?" Gregor asked easily as he ran.

"I'm worried about Mel," I admitted. "And Athena."

Gregor's eyes narrowed and he zeroed in on his house. Then, he took off. And I mean took off. He was still in his running shoes and clothes. Roosevelt and I were left eating his dust.

"Gregor! Wait!"

But when Gregor kicks like that, there's no catching him. I could only sprint along behind and hope for the best.

By the time I reached his front porch, gasping and clutching a sweat-soaked copy of *Pandora's Book*, Gregor was nowhere to be seen. For a second, I stood in the shade of the small porch, doubled over, trying to suck in air, while Roosevelt loped up the driveway. The guy may have led charges into battle and been on a few hunting expeditions, but he was no match for Gregor's and my speed.

"Your friend," Roosevelt said, panting, "he went around back?"

I shrugged helplessly. "He was too fast." I swung my head around but saw no sign of Gregor anywhere in the yard or by the front window of his house. "I lost him."

"Do we know how many of them there are?" Roosevelt asked, pulling a few gold cylinders from a pocket and sliding them into the side of his gun. My stomach somersaulted. He was putting ammo in there. For real.

I shook my head. "I only ever heard the one German guy. But there could be more, I guess."

Roosevelt tapped his gun to make sure everything was in place and stepped up onto the porch. He slid between me and the front door. "Are you quite familiar with the layout of this dwelling, son?"

"Yes, sir."

"Excellent." Roosevelt kept his voice low. "You'll

stay behind me then but direct me where to go. Do we have a location?"

"The GPS showed him to be in the back of the house."

I realized at that moment that Athena wasn't barking. My stomach somersaulted again. *Please God*, I prayed, *for Gregor's sake, let that dog be okay.*

Roosevelt twisted the knob on the front door. It turned easily, and the door swung open. He slid quietly into the room. My heart pounding so loudly that I could hear it in my ears, I followed.

The family room was dark. The front curtains were drawn and no lights were on. The only light came from the kitchen windows in the back of the house, so everything was dim and shadowy. Instantly, it became much tougher for me to see. Even still, I could make out that the room was a mess. But the room was always a mess. Nobody in Gregor's family is very neat. Surprising, considering how much Gregor likes order. I guess this was one area where he allowed some chaos in his life.

Roosevelt picked his way over books and blankets,

newspapers and shoes, and I followed, both of us straining to hear any sound at all coming from the back of the house. It was dead silent. We poked our heads into the kitchen, but other than some dirty dishes, an empty milk carton, and an overflowing trash can, it was clean. Roosevelt looked at me. I nodded my head toward the back hallway. He raised his rifle and slowly started making his way toward the darkened hall entrance. I gripped *Pandora's Book* tightly under my arm and followed.

We'd gone only about three or four steps, when a loud *thud!* shook the house.

"Move!" yelled someone from a back room.

A girl.

Mel.

I bolted. Pushing past Roosevelt (whose reaction time was questionable for someone so highly decorated), I sprinted down the hall toward Gregor's room, where I'd heard Mel's shout come from. I threw my shoulder against the closed door and fell into Gregor's room.

Like every other room in the house, it was a

mess. Clothes everywhere. Papers, books, shoes, dirty socks. His bed was stripped clean of sheets and was instead a tangled mess of pillows, blankets, and pajamas.

At first I didn't see them. My eyes were having trouble adjusting to the bright light of the room after the dimness of the rest of the house. I blinked once. Twice. Swung my gaze around the room.

"Gregor!"

"Mel's here," he answered tonelessly. "Athena's not."

And then I saw him. Squatting down between the bed and the closet. Gregor was leaning over Mel, untying her hands, which were lashed behind her back with what looked like a belt and then hitched to one post of Gregor's bed.

Mel rubbed her wrists and sprang to her feet. She looked ticked off.

"Snap, crackle, pop! What took you so long?" she asked, tucking her hair behind her ears, her eyes wide and flashing.

I blinked again and pushed my glasses up my nose.

"You're welcome," I said.

Gregor stood up. "Athena wasn't out back, either, Spencer." His eyes darted nervously.

Roosevelt came into the room but wrinkled his nose in distaste.

"They've made a royal mess of the place, I'm afraid," he said.

Mel barked a laugh. "Hardly."

In one smooth movement, she hopped onto Gregor's bed. "Quick! He escaped that way!" She already had one leg out Gregor's open window. Apparently Evil Dude had pushed the screen out of it.

Gregor was frozen by his closet, his fingers tapping on his thighs.

"Where's Athena?" he asked quietly. "She wasn't in the kitchen, Spencer. She's always in the kitchen."

Jeez, had he toured the house already?

"Come on!" Mel urged.

"Mel!" I yelled. "Stop a minute, okay? We have to think about what we're doing! We're all safe now! Maybe we can call the police or something."

"We can't waste any time, Spencer!" Mel said, dropping to the ground outside. She looked back at me through the open window. "You don't get it, do you? What he's going to do?"

"Where's Athena?" Gregor asked again, his voice rising.

Roosevelt was surveying each of us, seemingly disappointed that he didn't get to use his gun.

"Are we going to go after our esteemed foe?" he asked.

I took a step toward Mel. "I have *Pandora's Book*," I said. "What can he do?" I showed her the large book under my arm.

Mel laughed, but it was a mocking laugh. A *you-don't-know-anything* laugh.

"He has *Pandora's Other Book*, you idiot," she said.

"What?"

But something nagged at my brain. *Pandora's Other Book*. Where had I seen that?

Then it hit me. Frank DiCarlo/Al Capone. He was carrying *Pandora's Other Book* when he came to see me that day.

I got a funny feeling in my stomach. A funny, "not good" feeling.

"I need to find Athena, Spencer," Gregor muttered urgently.

I glanced at Gregor, but knew he would have to wait a second. I climbed slowly onto the bed so I could face Mel through the open window.

"This *Other Book*," I said. "What's in it?"

"Ed never told you?"

I shook my head.

"It's the exact opposite of *Pandora's Book*. The yin to its yang. *Pandora's Book* is filled with all the remarkable people who ever walked this earth. People who made an impact. A positive impact. *Pandora's Other Book* is filled with people who did the exact opposite."

"So wait . . . ," I said, my mind trying to process what she was saying. "If *Pandora's Book* has people like Martin Luther King Jr. and Teddy Roosevelt, then *Pandora's Other Book* has people like . . ."

Mel nodded slowly, her eyes flat. "Hitler. 'Machine Gun' Kelly. Osama Bin Laden."

I was already shaking my head. "No, that's not possible. I know who has this *Other Book*. It's Frank

DiCarlo, or Al Capone, or whoever he is. I just saw him earlier today. And I saw him with *Pandora's Other Book* yesterday, so there's no way that . . ."

"Frank DiCarlo doesn't have *Pandora's Other Book*, Spencer." Mel's voice was hard, insistent. "You need to listen to me, okay? Heinrich—the German guy who shot at us earlier—*he* has *Pandora's Other Book*. And he has plans to use it. If possible, he wants to get his hands on that book, too." She pointed at *Pandora's Book*. "But don't you see? We have to stop him. He's evil. And he's got Ed."

When she said that last sentence, her voice cracked. She looked away.

"He has Ed?" My words were barely above a whisper.

She nodded, and I saw her swipe at her eyes quickly before looking at me again. "Heinrich can't operate these books by himself, see? Whatever magic it has, he can't just make it work. He needs Ed to do it for him. But Spencer . . ." She swallowed. "Ed's old. Heinrich knows this. He'll need somebody younger." She looked at me pointedly.

My bones liquefied. "Me?" I whispered.

"Where's Athena?" Gregor asked from behind me. His voice was tense now. He was heading rapidly toward a full meltdown.

Mel's eyes turned toward Gregor and then back to me. Something darkened in them. "Oh, snap," she muttered. To me, very quietly, she asked, "Who's Athena?"

"His dog."

She closed her eyes and let out a long breath of air.

"He took her." I could barely hear her words. "He took the dog, Spencer."

And that's when I got mad. I didn't know who this guy was. But Athena means everything to Gregor. *Everything.* And there was no reason to take that dog. Ed and Mel and I were somehow wrapped up in this crazy mess. But Athena?

Anger was building in my chest like a campfire slowly igniting.

"Where's he going, Mel?" I asked, already pulling off my backpack. If we were going to go after this guy, I had to be prepared. Which meant putting *Pandora's Book* safely in my backpack and taking out something more useful to fight with. At least with an airsoft gun in my hands, I'd look more like Jason Bourne, right? Jason Bourne with glasses.

"I'm not sure, but I have some guesses," she said.

I was zipping up my backpack and getting ready to sling it on my back when Gregor stood up from his crouched position.

"SPENCER!" he yelled. "I WANT TO KNOW WHERE ATHENA IS!"

His hands were balled up, and his breathing was shallow. I glanced over at Mel. Her eyes were wide as saucers. Colonel Roosevelt took a step backward toward the door.

"Listen, G.," I said, in what I hoped was a calming and soothing voice, "I'm sure she's fine, but . . ."

Gregor sank down into a crouch and started muttering to himself. He was curled into a tight ball, eyes closed. I knew, then, we might have to leave him. But I couldn't leave him alone.

I closed my eyes. *Dear God,* I prayed, *I'm not sure what to do on this one. A little help?*

When I opened my eyes, Mel was looking at me impatiently. Roosevelt was regarding me thoughtfully. Gregor was still rocking on the floor. They were all waiting for me to make a decision. But what in the heck was I supposed to do? I hadn't asked to be commander in chief of this mission. I hadn't *asked* for this mission at all!

I looked around Gregor's disaster of a room and spied a picture of him and Athena on his dresser. It was half covered with an inside-out running sock, but instinctively I grabbed the photo, flinging the sock to the floor. I knelt by Gregor.

"Hey, G.," I said softly. "Open your eyes, buddy."

Gregor continued his keening. It was like he didn't hear me. I swallowed the lump in my throat and tried again.

"I'm going to find Athena, okay? Maybe that guy just let her out. Or maybe he took her with him. But I'm going to go get her. Remember what you said to me in my room? About focusing on what's ahead? I'm gonna do that. I'm gonna focus on getting Athena back here safely."

I pushed the picture frame into Gregor's hand and started to stand up. I turned to Mel.

"Can I use your phone? I gotta call his mom to come get—"

"I'm coming."

I looked down at Gregor in astonishment. He was uncurling himself and standing, though he was still shaking, and his fingers were tapping madly.

"Dude, are you sure that . . . ?"

"I'm coming," Gregor said more firmly. He gently set the picture of him and Athena down on his bed. "She's my dog. After you, she's my best friend. She would protect me. So I'm coming."

I was speechless. Slowly, I slung my backpack onto my back and tucked the airsoft gun up under my arm.

"Okay, then." I gulped. "I guess we're ready to, uh, go kick some butt or something."

It was the most pitiful war cry in the history of the world. But it got Gregor moving toward the window. And Mel kind of smiled . . . I guess.

As I dropped to the ground outside, I looked back into Gregor's room.

"Colonel Roosevelt, sir? You coming?" I called.

Roosevelt grinned. "And miss out on the butt-kicking? I think not."

Gregor's neighbor was watering her roses as we let ourselves out the side gate and started down the street, following Mel. She did a double take when she saw us and sprayed her own cat—who was less than pleased by the shower.

I can only imagine what she saw. Gregor, trying to look brave, his hands resolutely balled at his sides, his mouth twisted into a grim frown as he quietly recited the names of Greek gods. Mel—beautiful and sure-of-herself Mel, who had no business hanging out with Gregor and me. Tall Roosevelt in his buckskin leather, clutching his rifle, looking like he belonged in another century because, oh yeah, he *did*. And me, pushing my sweaty glasses up my nose, gripping my airsoft gun and trying not to puke all over the back of Mel's Nikes.

Together, somehow, we were going to take down a bad guy and rescue Ed and save the world. I closed my eyes and said a prayer.

CHAPTER 16
THE MYSTERY
STARTS TO UNRAVEL

For a while, I walked next to Gregor, but a person can only answer the question "Do you think Athena's okay?" so many times. I left Gregor to his Greek gods and jogged to walk by Roosevelt instead.

"So you think we can take this guy?" I asked.

I threw the airsoft gun over my shoulder, the way Roosevelt had his rifle, and tried to copy his swagger. The gun kept whacking me in the head, and after about thirty seconds my calves started burning from bouncing on my toes so much. Plus, Roosevelt had launched into a long-winded answer about tactical maneuvers and preparedness and wrongheadedness. I found myself reluctantly slinking back toward Mel.

I fell in step beside her and said nothing. Crazily, I could smell her. Why was it that, even though she'd done a whole lot of running and probably fought like crazy against the Evil Dude, she still smelled like baby powder and sugar cookies? Girls are amazing that way—their ability to smell good at all times.

Finally, I couldn't take it anymore.

"How come you're here?" I asked, gripping the airsoft gun and training my eyes on the sidewalk ahead.

Mel snorted. "Same reason you are. To get back the books. You know, save the world from evil and all that." She waved her hand dismissively.

"No, I mean, why are you *here*? How did you know I'd need your help?" I looked over at her then, noting how the sun caught her hair and lit up her head like a halo. She didn't wear earrings, didn't even have the holes for them. She had a small but shiny scar just above her right eye.

For a long time, Mel didn't answer. I could see her jaw clenching and unclenching. Behind us, Gregor continued to mutter his slew of gods.

"Ed called me," she said finally. She sighed and

seemed to make up her mind about something. "Right after you left. He told me that he'd given you *Pandora's Book*. But he said he was worried. Worried that he was being watched. He wanted me to know in case something happened. This morning, I had a bad feeling. I cut out of school after lunch and headed toward his place. But when I got there, there was all sorts of activity going on, and I *knew*. I knew Heinrich had gotten him. So I decided to find you instead."

"But your parents?" I asked. "Do they know you're here? Aren't they worried?"

She snorted again. "My parents are likely in a different hemisphere right now, tracking down stuff that belonged to famous dead people. Ironic, isn't it?" She gestured toward Roosevelt with her chin. "I'm here, having a merry old time with Teddy Roosevelt, while my dear old Mom and Dad would offer an arm and a leg—probably mine—to have that gun he's carrying in their collection." She laughed, but it was a hard-edged laugh.

My heart ached for her suddenly.

"Why didn't Ed give *Pandora's Book* to you?"

It had been bothering me ever since she'd said she knew about the books. Why had he given it to me, when Mel seemed so much more capable? So much better equipped to guard it than me?

Again she didn't speak for a long time. She dropped her chin and walked along silently. I was sure I had crossed some sort of line and upset her.

"He tried," she finally said, so softly, I almost couldn't hear her.

"What?" I was startled.

"He tried," she said louder. "But I couldn't make it work. The book didn't want me, Spencer." Even from the side, I could see her face was pained. "I should have guessed it, you know? My parents might not be the best people to . . . well, anyway." She sucked in a deep breath. "The book didn't want me."

I swallowed. For a moment, I thought about reaching out to squeeze her hand. Telling her that she was amazing. That the book was stupid. Her parents were stupid. But I didn't reach out, and I said nothing.

We walked the rest of the way in silence.

Finally, we reached a one-story seventies-style building that had a wide set of glass double doors and a wheelchair-friendly ramp that wound up to it. An American flag waved in the breeze above our heads. And to our left was a bulletin board jam-packed with fliers that said things like "BINGO: Thursdays at 7:30" and "Need to Jump Start that Old Heart? Come to Rhonda's Chair Aerobics Class Every Wednesday." The parking lot out front was loaded with Buicks and Chryslers, most of them older than me.

Mel stopped us and looked around as if she expected something bad to happen right then.

"This is where Evil German Guy hangs out?" I asked, not bothering to keep the surprise from my voice.

Mel glared at me like I'd suddenly grown an extra ear. "Evil German Guy?" she asked, and kind of half snorted, half laughed.

I felt myself turning red. "What else should I call him? Sir? Mr. Guy Who Is Trying to Kill Us?"

Mel continued to look at me intently. "I thought

you'd have this all figured out by now. You seemed so, I don't know, smart."

Her voice dripped with sarcasm.

All my warm feelings toward her vanished. I didn't know whether to be ticked or embarrassed. I threw up my hands. "Forgive me for not having my *genius* in order right now, but I've been a little busy trying to track down *your* butt and make sure you were okay. I haven't had a lot of time to ponder the five Ws and the H of this whole day yet."

Mel started laughing and then looked at me with interest. "You crack me up, Spencer," she said, then she spun around to face the doors of the senior center.

"He teaches German to some of the old folks here twice a week," she said as she eyed the building like she was looking for another way in. "As far as I can tell anyway."

I'd been here once with my mom. She'd taught a yoga class to the seniors in this building a few years back. I was sick and had to stay home from school, but apparently not sick enough that she couldn't drag me to yoga class with her. Do you know what happens when seventy- and eighty-year-old women try to do yoga poses? I'll tell you what happens: They fart. Repeatedly. And somehow, through this session of twisted old bodies and passing gas, I was supposed to NOT LAUGH.

It was almost dinnertime now, which meant that somewhere in that building a whole herd of seniors was shuffling toward a full buffet of mushy meatloaf, mashed potatoes, and boiled carrots. Pudding, probably, for dessert. Everything all nice and soft with all those dentures and exposed gums. Blech.

And according to Mel, Evil German Guy—Heinrich—was somewhere in there, too.

"How do you know?"

Mel shrugged. "I started tailing him a few days ago after Ed kind of let it slip that this guy might be bad news. I noticed that he spent a lot of time here, when he wasn't following you or DiCarlo around."

I gulped. "He's been following me around?"

She nodded. "Since you started hanging out with Ed. And since I've been following *him*."

I got a nasty feeling in the pit of my stomach—
like when you drink milk too fast. How could I not
have noticed someone spying on me?

It explained, though, how he knew where Gregor lived. And how he knew that if he wanted us
to come after him, he should kidnap Athena. He'd
been watching us.

Gregor joined us. His hands were twitchy, and he
was rocking back and forth on his heels. He was also
mumbling under his breath, mostly about Athena.
But, all in all, he was hanging in there pretty well.

"You think he took Athena in there?" Gregor
asked quietly, pointing at the front doors of the
senior center.

Mel looked doubtful. "I've never seen anyone take
a dog in, Gregor. But I don't know. Maybe."

My stomach felt like it had rocks in it. If Athena
wasn't with him anymore, what had he done with
her? Why would he hurt an innocent dog like that?

"He's a bad man, isn't he, Mel?" Gregor asked.

Mel was nodding without looking at Gregor. "I'm

not sure he was always bad, Gregor. But somewhere along the way, yes, he turned into the same kind of evil monster that his commanding officer was."

Roosevelt was pacing behind us, unaware or unconcerned with our conversation. I think he simply wanted to go kick some butt. I, however, was tired of not knowing who my enemy was.

"Who is he, Mel? The guy we're after?"

She took a deep breath. "You won't know him from any history books. He's not even supposed to be alive anymore, though somehow he's managed not to age at all since he's been out of the book. It was all a terrible mistake. . . ."

At that moment an ear-piercing siren, coming from somewhere inside of the senior center, cut her off. Mel's eyes widened.

"Snap, crackle, pop!" she said, placing her hand on my arm and squeezing.

The siren kept screaming its alarm. The front doors of the senior center flew open, and a parade of people—shuffling, limping, hunched-over folks in all manner of cardigans and soft-soled shoes—started filing out. Gregor clamped his hands over both ears and squinched his eyes shut in pain.

But all I could concentrate on was Mel's hand. The way every nerve in my body seemed to zero in on those five lovely fingers of hers.

Until she yanked me down toward the pavement. Hard. And the last thing I saw before I went eye-to-eye with the cement was the look Mel gave me.

Fear. Mel was scared to death.

CHAPTER 17
THINGS (PREDICTABLY) GO FROM BAD TO WORSE

Out of the corner of my eye, I saw Roosevelt grab Gregor and drag him off to the side of the building and out of harm's way. I was too stunned to move, but some kind of survival instinct kicked in, I guess, and I threw my body on top of my backpack to protect *Pandora's Book*. My glasses slid off and hit the pavement several feet away. The world was suddenly one big, giant blur.

"He's here, Spencer." Mel's voice sounded very far away. "He saw us. Stay down."

I was pretty sure I was going to die. Trampled to death by Keds and Easy Spirits.

Someone inside the building screamed. Or maybe it was me.

"You kids hold still!" Roosevelt hollered out from somewhere.

He shouldn't have bothered. I covered my head with my hands and closed my eyes.

"Spencer!" I felt Mel's hand slide into mine.

She squeezed. I squeezed back. I couldn't see her, but I peeked open one eye and tried to smile in her direction to show her I was fearless and alive. Okay, just alive.

"We've got to get out of here. Stay right behind me, got it?"

She let go of my hand, and I saw her raise up on all fours and start crawling slowly toward the side of the building. I had to scooch my backpack along underneath me, but I tried to follow.

The siren continued to blare. I didn't know if there was a fire inside that building, or if this was someone's idea of a prank. Somehow, though, I suspected that Evil German Guy was behind this slow-motion stampede, this swarm of agitated old people. And it was designed to trap us.

I could hear a police siren way, way off in the distance.

Yes, this was Heinrich's doing. He had faked a heart attack or pulled the fire alarm or something. And he was probably headed toward us. And *Pandora's Book*.

More and more feet were running past us. Or maybe hobbling is a better word, since the feet that were close enough for me to see seemed to be in loafers and belonged to the over-seventy crowd. Someone stabbed the end of their cane down on the back of my hand.

"Oww!" I hollered, but no one heard or cared.

I crawled a few more paces, staying close to Mel's Nikes. Then, off to my left, I could just make out my glasses. There were more people filing past us now, frantic and scared, some of them crying out for help, most of them paying no attention to the two kids who crept along on the ground below.

On the one hand, this was good. It meant we actually had a little protection.

On the other, it meant my glasses were about to be toast.

I snaked out my hand, barely dodging tennis balls stuck to the bottom of some lady's walker. My fingers were just brushing the thick frames of my glasses . . . so close . . . one more inch . . .

Something hard landed against my ribs. My right side erupted in pain and for a moment I couldn't breathe. I collapsed and curled onto my side—everything forgotten except trying to relieve the searing pain in my side. Someone had kicked me. Kicked me *hard*.

"Spencer! NO!" My hazy mind managed to decipher Mel's voice. "The backpack, Spencer!"

I squinted up to see who or what had attacked me but could only make out large and fuzzy shapes. Throbs of pain shot through my ribs. Before I could stop it, a huge spray of puke erupted from my mouth and landed on the pavement next to me.

"NO!" Mel screamed. Her fuzzy form rose up from the ground and lunged toward whoever had kicked me. There were grunts as I guessed she fought to prevent him from taking the backpack.

But then I saw him lift something long and pointed. High over his head he raised it.

With as much strength as I had, I screamed, "Mel! Look! Move!"

But it was too late. He brought it down against her. With a sickening crunch, it hit her in the side of her head, and she crumpled, falling on top of me, her head first hitting my legs and then lolling sideways to hit the pavement.

I felt sick again as I tried to reach her, struggling to roll over somehow, fighting the pain in my ribs, wincing with each movement.

The man laughed, standing over us for a moment, his blurry, dark form blocking everything else from view. Then he turned and fled, flinging a dark shape—my backpack, no doubt—over his shoulder. He disappeared into the crowd of seniors that was still flowing out of the center.

"Mel?" My voice wasn't much more than a whisper. I was fighting tears.

I reached for her and turned her head slightly so I could see her face. But everything was too blurry.

Someone knelt down next to us.

"What happened? Are you okay?"

I shook my head, unable to speak, and pointed at Mel.

"Oh, my God!" the woman said. She stood. "Someone call for help! Please! Call 9-1-1! This girl is bleeding!"

Within seconds, we were swarmed by people. Some tried to stop Mel's bleeding, find her pulse, check for other injuries. Some pushed me up to sitting until they realized that I, too, was injured. Then they just let me lie there and tried to keep me calm until the ambulance arrived.

At some point, the world started to go even fuzzier than it already was. I had so many questions. Where was Gregor? I hadn't seen him since the whole chaotic scene started. Did Roosevelt get him to safety? I didn't know.

But there was one thing I did know. I couldn't do this anymore. I couldn't fight. Heinrich could have

Pandora's Book. Take over the world for all I cared. It had to be someone else's problem.

Pain ricocheted through my body. My head felt like someone had taken a jackhammer to it. My ribs were searing, on fire. I cursed Ed for getting me into this mess. Mel for dragging me further into it than I wanted to go. And the German guy for being an *Evil* German Guy.

I didn't want them to, but the tears were starting. Tears of self-pity and fear. I had failed. Failed miserably. I couldn't protect Mel. I couldn't even keep a book from getting taken by a madman. I was so, so tired. I just wanted to be home. Listening to Molly giggle in the next room. Helping Gregor with his math homework.

Gregor.

Where was Gregor? Was he okay? Was he freaking out?

I could picture my friend, his fingers tapping like mad, his eyes darting around nervously, while he was reciting every Greek god he'd ever learned. He'd stayed by my side through this whole mess. Despite everything in him wanting to bolt, to shut down. He hadn't, though.

Why?

I swiped at the tears with the back of my hand.

Why had he stayed with me?

Sure, he loved history. The people in this book were seriously important to him. He would do anything to protect them. To keep *Pandora's Book* in good hands.

But that wasn't it. I knew that.

I'd needed him, and Athena had needed him. And so he'd stayed.

I looked over at Mel. I couldn't help her. But if she woke up and found out I'd given up, she was going to kill me. Failing was not an option to her. Giving up was unforgivable.

I knew what I had to do, even though I hated the thought of doing it.

I swallowed the pain that was choking me. I had to get out of there before the paramedics arrived. Because then I'd be tossed into an ambulance, jetted off to a hospital, and the guy with my backpack—and *Pandora's Book*—would be long gone by the time I was discharged. No, I had to move. *Now.*

I pushed myself up to my elbows. A wave of nausea crashed through my chest, but I pushed it back down. Most of the people around us were focused on Mel. Who lay unmoving on the sidewalk. I forced myself to look away from her. They'd help her, make sure she was okay.

I sat all the way up. Pain flooded my body. No doubt, he'd broken one of my ribs. I still couldn't see much without my glasses. And the airsoft gun I'd been carrying had been knocked from my hands when I'd dropped to the ground. With my good arm—the one that I could move without feeling as if my ribs were going to explode—I started feeling around on the ground nearby. Nothing.

I tried to roll over and crawl around. I knew at one point my glasses had been close. But in the stampede of all those old people's feet, they could have been crushed to smithereens by now and I would never know.

I crawled farther away from Mel, hoping, at the very least, that I could make my getaway. The police sirens were very loud now. The paramedics would be here any second.

"Spencer?"

Gregor. I wanted to cry with relief. He'd made it.

I leaned back onto my knees, letting my right arm cradle my throbbing rib cage. "Dude," I said softly, fighting back tears. "You're okay. What happened back there?"

I couldn't see Gregor's face, but I felt him press something into the palm of my hand. My glasses. Hurriedly, with my good arm, I managed to get them on my face again.

The scene was terrifying.

Gregor's face was ashen, and he was literally shaking so badly, I'm not sure how he was still standing. I didn't see Roosevelt anywhere nearby, but there were so many people around, it was hard to tell.

A small crowd—mostly workers from the senior center, it looked like—knelt around Mel. One held Mel's head in her lap. Another was taking her pulse.

A third, an older lady, was simply patting her hand and murmuring, "It'll be okay." Looking at Mel's face, it was hard to agree with her.

An ugly purple welt was already forming near Mel's right eye, and blood was seeping out of an inch-long gash there. The ground around Mel's head was spotted red, as were the clothes of the women helping Mel.

I turned away and swallowed.

"Did you see who did that to her?"

Gregor nodded, pools of tears welling up in the lower corners of his eyes. He was crouched next to me, rocking back and forth on his heels. He looked down at the ground.

I swallowed again. A lump rose in my throat.

"Gregor?" I said. He looked up again. "We'll get him."

But Gregor's stare was vacant.

"He hurt Athena. Mel. You," he muttered.

The paramedics were pushing their way through the crowd.

I forced myself up to my feet. For a second, the ground swam, and I had to reach out both hands to steady myself.

"We've got to get out of here before they start questioning us," I said to Gregor.

I turned one more time and glanced around. The alarm whined on. Senior citizens milled around, leaning on walkers, clustered in hunched-over groups, sending nervous glances toward Mel and me.

"Yeah, Gregor," I said, feeling anxious, "we've got to go *now*."

Gregor was still crouched on the ground, tapping and pulling his body ever tighter into a ball. He didn't move.

"He hurt Athena. Mel. You," he repeated.

Panic licked at my heart.

"Gregor," I said, trying to stay calm. "Come on, buddy. I need your help. Let's at least get out of here, and then we can talk about what we should do."

Gregor didn't stand up.

I glanced around. Where was Roosevelt?

I didn't see a tall guy in uniform with a rifle any-where. Maybe he'd taken off after Evil German Guy. Good, I hoped he was kicking his butt.

I took a deep breath. My ribs were on fire. Stand-ing up was painful. I could see the paramedics start-ing to bend over Mel. A police car was rolling up to the curb.

It was now or never.

"Gregor." I reached down with my good arm and touched his shoulder. He drew back.

Okay. I was going to have to go without him.

But . . . where?

Someone tapped me on the shoulder. My heart sank. Too late. We'd waited too long, and now we were going to have to go through twenty questions with the cops.

I spun around.

"Young man, I believe I might be of some help in this situation."

He still wore his white toga, though it and his beard looked like they needed to be introduced to some soap. Soon.

"Socrates?"

Gregor began unfolding himself from his crouched position.

Socrates smiled. "You see, your friend Ed is a good friend of mine, too—taught me to play chess, you know—so when I learned he was in trouble, well, I decided to use my understanding of good and evil to try to help his cause."

Gregor's shaking had stopped. He was looking at his idol with awe.

"Socrates," he breathed. "You're okay."

"Yes, my wise young man. But I do believe I will need your help for this next part."

Gregor stared for a second. Then he nodded.

"Well, then, my good friends," Socrates said. "I believe we've got a job to do."

CHAPTER 18

WE MEET A REALLY COOL HOMELESS LADY

There are places in every town where kids understand not to go. Unless they want to get beat up, offered pot, or stabbed. The "Other Side of the Tracks." The "Wrong Side of Town." You probably know right where I'm talking about in your town, and you just got the willies thinking about it.

In my neighborhood, it's this creepy overgrown field next to our local mountains where a set of train tracks runs. Crisscrossing overtop are two more sets of train tracks running along a rickety metal bridge. Underneath this train trestle, the misfits of society congregate. Drug addicts. Homeless guys. Teenagers wanting to stir up trouble. And occasionally, save-the-world do-gooders like my mom, dragging her two children and bags of cast-off clothing and blankets behind us.

Yeah, I've been there. It had creeped me out then, and it creeped me out now.

I was guessing it had to be about six o'clock. The sun was dipping below the mountains. As is typical in late April in Southern California, a chilly mist was settling up against the nearby mountains. I was still wearing my running clothes, little goose bumps breaking out on my legs and arms. Plus, the ribs on my right side were still on fire. Yep, one was definitely broken or else really, really badly bruised. I was trying to take shallow breaths but even that hurt.

Socrates and Gregor were walking along ahead of me like they were old chums. Every once in a while I caught a word or two, and odds were they weren't strategizing about the battle ahead. No, they were philosophizing. About life. And good and evil. And whether death by drinking hemlock was worse than being hit by a bus. And of course, Gregor was asking Socrates if he'd seen a large yellow dog. It should have annoyed the heck out of me. But I had other things to be worried about.

Pandora's Book was gone. In the hands of a very, very bad guy. Ed was still missing. Probably in the hands of the very same bad guy. And Mel was on her way to the hospital. She was going to wake up with a pretty nasty bruise over one eye and a headache for which Tylenol was not going to cut it. Gregor's dog was still MIA and maybe dead.

I hung my head. On all fronts, I had screwed things up. Royally.

Why had Ed ever given me *Pandora's Book*? Why did he think I could handle this responsibility? Couldn't he see that I was just a nearly blind loser who couldn't even protect his best friend's *dog* from getting hurt?

I could see the glow of a homeless man's fire pit up ahead. When my mom, sister, and I had come before, we'd been surprised to see how these guys dragged the insides of old washing machines out here and used them as fire pits. It wasn't exactly safe, considering how dry the brush was on the nearby hillsides, but I guess it kept these guys warm on cold nights. And I noticed that somebody had actually cleared most of the brush off the hillsides now, so maybe there was an unspoken agreement between the authorities and the vagrants.

I had no clue why Socrates had led us out here. My mom was going to be worried sick when she realized that Gregor and I weren't showing up for dinner. Mrs. Chandramouli was going to freak when she saw Gregor's open window and found Athena missing. What made me think it was a good idea to follow a guy in a toga out here—to the outskirts of town at dusk? I sighed. Another bad decision.

Socrates led us closer to the lone homeless guy huddled near the fire. He wore a long brown woolen coat with a sweatshirt underneath. The hood on the sweatshirt was pulled way up so that you couldn't see his face. On his feet were large black military-style boots, laced up nearly to mid-shin. Though his hands were out toward the fire, they were wrapped in worn black knit gloves.

Socrates was looking all around as if he expected

someone or something else to be here. I followed his gaze, but all I saw were the deepening shadows created by the train trestle overhead and piles of dusty, frayed clothes and blankets—some of which had probably been donated by yours truly.

"Socrates?" I asked, and found that speaking really hurt my ribs. I grunted in pain and held my side. "Why are we here?"

Socrates didn't answer. He brought a finger up to his beard and stroked it gently while his eyes took on a faraway look.

He walked up to the guy by the fire. "Phylis?" he said gently.

I glanced at Gregor and saw the same surprise on his face. Under all those clothes was a woman. She didn't look up but continued to stare at the flames and rub her lips together in an odd way.

"He's here, Phylis," Socrates said. "I know he his."

Socrates reached out and touched her shoulder very gently. She jumped away from his touch but made no eye contact. She wrung her hands, rhythmically, and rubbed her lips together—back and forth, back and forth.

"Phylis," he said again, slowly and calmly. "I'd like you to meet someone." Socrates looked back at Gregor and motioned for him to come forward. "Phylis. This is Gregor. Gregor, this is Phylis."

For an odd moment, no one moved. Phylis continued to squeeze her gloved hands together and do that funny thing with her lips. Gregor stood uncomfortably, rigid and straight, his fingers tapping on his thighs. I looked at one and then the other. And I knew.

Phylis was autistic. Just like Gregor. An adult with autism. Probably no way to find a job or an apartment. No way to pay bills or buy groceries to make dinner. So she'd ended up here.

Tears pooled in my eyes. I couldn't let this happen to Gregor. He's too smart. Too awesome. He'd shown that today. No way would I ever let him end up abandoned like this. I shook my head to clear it.

"Gregor," Socrates said, quietly, "my friend, Phylis, is very, very wise. She is a master at mental computations. Go ahead, Gregor. Give her some numbers."

Gregor looked back at me uncertainly. I didn't know what to tell him. I didn't understand what was going on any more than he did.

"Socrates," I said, "we really need to hurry and find *Pandora's Book*. What does this have to do with . . . ?"

Socrates held up his hand and my words dribbled off. I shrugged at Gregor as if to say, *Sure, go ahead.*

Gregor squeezed his eyes closed to concentrate. Numbers are not his thing. Unless they're dates or running times, Gregor stays away from numbers. I had a good idea how he was going to come up with the numbers he needed right then.

"1939," he said. *World War II breaks out*, I thought.

"1492," he said. *Columbus sails the ocean blue*, I finished silently.

"And 1969." *The year we landed a man on the moon.*

Without pausing, Phylis muttered, "Five thousand four hundred." Almost like she couldn't help herself.

I grinned. This woman was good.

But I still wasn't sure how this was going to help us find Heinrich.

Socrates was smiling. "Phylis, you never cease to amaze me," he said. "Now, Gregor, look at that bridge up there." Gregor looked.

"How high off the ground do you think it is?"

Gregor looked up at the bridge and down at the ground. Up again and down again. I knew what he was thinking. He was thinking he had absolutely no clue. He sucks at numbers. I told you that.

But Phylis knew. "Thirty feet, six and a half inches," she said in her weird monotone voice. She didn't look up.

I didn't know if she was right, but something in me said she was. Exactly right. And that she'd never taken out a ruler and measured.

Gregor moved closer to me. "Ask her if she's seen Athena, Spencer," he whispered to me urgently.

I cleared my throat.

"Um, excuse me . . ." I started, but Socrates silenced me with a raised hand.

"Phylis," Socrates said, staring at her wrinkled profile. "I need to know where he is. How many steps should I take, Phylis?"

Her eyes were unblinking. She stared only at the fire.

Socrates sighed. "*Truth always lies beneath the shadows of our existence.*"

Gregor looked up at Socrates, eyes shining in respect. In a monotone that matched Phylis's, he said, "But the philosopher's job is to show everyone how much they don't know about life."

Socrates smiled. "Well done, boy."

Then he turned back to Phylis. "Please, my dear woman. He means to harm these two boys. And more than that—the whole of society. The good of the world. But you can help us, Phylis. Tell me where he hides. I know you watch. I know he's asked you to watch and promised not to harm you. But he is not a good man. You know that as well as do I."

Phylis did not look at Socrates but her hands slowed in their wringing. Her lips stopped their rhythmic tightening and untightening. Now they just clamped together firmly.

Then she muttered, "The path. The path by the rock. Four hundred and six steps. Another path to the left. Six hundred thirty-two steps to the big tree."

She sucked in a breath, let it out, and then her hands started wringing fast as lightning, and her lips started moving big-time.

Socrates smiled. "Thank you, Phylis. You have done much good, kind woman."

He turned to the two of us. "Are you ready, then?"

Were we ready?

We had no weapons of any kind. Gregor was terrified and probably on his last moments before a major breakdown. Socrates's biggest strength was tossing out questions—none of which could take down an Evil Dude. And I was struggling to breathe through a broken rib.

"Let's go," I said with as much enthusiasm as I could muster.

My legs were already starting to tremble. There

was a battle in my future. I could feel it. And I didn't know if I'd survive it.

Right then, Phylis finally turned her head away from the fire and spoke. She looked directly at me. Her eyes were gray, and the firelight glinting off of them gave her an eerie, ghostly appearance. "Two books. One gun. One dog. Two prisoners."

She paused, and in that second I realized what she was doing: giving us an inventory of what Heinrich had. The two books: *Pandora's Book* and *Pandora's Other Book*. His nasty gun. Athena, Gregor's dog. And his two prisoners: Ed and probably DiCarlo.

Phylis pulled her lips in tightly. "Still missing one thing."

And she raised her gloved hand and pointed it right at me.

CHAPTER 19
HOW TO DEFEAT AN EVIL GERMAN GUY (IT'S NOT AS EASY AS IT SOUNDS)

I didn't count every step, but it sure felt like we'd taken about six hundred and thirty-two. All of them uphill. I was panting, tired, and pretty close to passing out.

In other words, in great shape for taking on an Evil German Guy.

And I could see that there was indeed a BIG tree.

As we neared Heinrich's hideout, we slowed down and crept into the shadows so he wouldn't know we were there. I was having a really hard time seeing now, since the light was nearly gone and my eyes were about done. It helped that Socrates was still in a white toga-like thing, which isn't exactly stealth material. He was like a beacon among all the other indistinct shapes.

Gregor and I were still in our running clothes. And freezing. My teeth chattered and I could see Gregor was shaking, too. But Gregor shakes a lot. Hard to tell if it was from the cold.

We huddled behind a large bush, trying not to snap any twigs to alert our enemy, and considered our next move.

"Do we just rush in there and demand that he give us back the books?" I asked Socrates, trying to keep my body warm by pulling myself into a tight ball. My ribs didn't like that so much. I groaned.

Socrates stroked his beard. "What do *you* think is our best move here, young friend?"

I rolled my eyes. I'd forgotten that Socrates became very un-useful in these situations. He was way too big on answering a question with a question. Which is great if you are having a discussion in history class. Not so good if you are trying to *not die*.

I closed my eyes. *Think, Spencer. What would*

Roosevelt do in this situation? He'd probably barrel in there and demand the books; but then again, he'd have a gun to barrel in with. I had nothing, nada; Evil German Guy had swiped my backpack at the senior center, and I'd never found my airsoft gun.

Okay. We could wait until he went to sleep and then try to sneak in and take the books. That wasn't a bad plan. I could leave Gregor and Socrates here and tiptoe over there myself. That way, they wouldn't be in danger at all.

"Here's my idea," I whispered, leaning my head toward them.

Just then a loud *snap!* in the underbrush caused all three of us to jump. My heart started hammering. Something or someone was coming up the same path we had used.

"Duck down," I whispered and grabbed Gregor to pull him to the ground next to me. My ribs screamed out in protest.

For the next few seconds, we didn't breathe. We could hear footsteps on the path. It was definitely a person, not an animal, based on the steady pounding.

But it was too dark to make out a shape, and I was pretty close to blind anyway. I prayed that whoever it was, he was on our side.

The footsteps grew closer and then, as they neared our bush, stopped. There was a click, like a gun being cocked. I froze.

What if it was Evil German Guy, and he knew we were here? I pressed Gregor down farther and tried to get between him and the path.

But Gregor was having none of it.

"Ow!" he yelped quietly. "Let me up, Spencer!"

My heart literally stopped beating, and I felt the blood leave my limbs. Numbness filled the far reaches of my body. We were going to die.

Except that whoever was on the path didn't take aim and fire. He took a tentative step toward our bush and leaned in.

"Spencer?"

It was Roosevelt. I'd know that clipped speech anywhere. My body grew numb again, but this time from relief. I rolled off Gregor and felt my ribs yelp.

"It's us, Roosevelt," I said quietly and tried to stand up without barfing.

Gregor poked his head out so Roosevelt could see him. Roosevelt ducked into the bushes with us, making sure not to disturb any branches or twigs beneath his feet. For a guy as big as he was, he was surprisingly agile.

"Ah, good to see you lads again!" Roosevelt said quietly, clapping me on my right shoulder. I winced in pain and bit my bottom lip. "You know, then, that this is the clandestine hideaway of our adversary?"

Through clenched teeth, I mentally translated what he said: this is where Evil German Guy was hiding out.

"How did you . . . get here?" Sharps stabs of pain racked my abdomen.

"Have you seen Athena?" asked Gregor eagerly.

"I followed the beastly fellow as soon as he bludgeoned that poor girl and made off with your book. He led me right here. I was farther down the path, tucked in among the foliage, when I saw the three of you come traipsing through a few minutes ago. I deduced then that it might be high time for a little ambush of our German friend." Roosevelt laughed merrily. He was all too ready to kick butt.

I was all too *not*.

"But alas, he did not have a canine companion, dear boy," Roosevelt said to Gregor.

"He's got a gun," I said, still holding my side and trying to swallow the pain. I felt like I might faint at any minute. "And two guys he's kidnapped."

"All the more reason to go in now, then, lad," Roosevelt said definitively. He held up his rifle and grinned.

I looked back at Socrates. He looked a little uncertain at the idea of a gun battle. I think he preferred to have a battle of the minds. Or a war of words. But I didn't think Heinrich was going to go for that.

Gregor looked like he might throw up. He was inching backward toward the path, like he might want to make a run for it. I can't say I blamed him.

"Gregor," I said softly, "you don't have to do this. Roosevelt and I can handle it. You stay with Socrates."

"But Athena," he muttered nervously, his hands fluttering by his thighs.

"We'll get her," I promised, though I wasn't sure how.

His head was shaking back and forth. I couldn't see his eyes in the darkness, but I was convinced we were heading toward a meltdown.

"Have to get Athena," he said with rising panic. "Have to get Athena."

"Gregor." I tried to shush him without reaching for him. He was making me nervous, the way he was backing up into the path, in full view of anyone who might walk along. And he was getting louder and more agitated. "Please, Gregor."

"Have to get Athena," he said one more time at full volume.

"Vell, zhen come and get her, *mein junger freund*," said a deep German voice behind him.

The voice alone sent a shiver up my spine.

Gregor spun around to face our enemy. Roosevelt moved toward Gregor and raised his rifle.

"Don't move! Nobody moves!" Roosevelt called out.

Heinrich laughed. Quickly, he reached forward, and before anyone could react, he grabbed Gregor's arm and tried to yank him forward.

Bad move, touching Gregor. Especially after stealing his dog.

Gregor's reaction was instant and instinctive. He did the same thing he would have done to me or you or the Queen of England. He smacked Heinrich in the face and then kicked him hard in the shin. And then he bolted. Toward the big tree and Athena, who we could now hear barking in the distance.

For a second, we were all stunned. Heinrich buckled, grabbing his shins and hollering up a storm, using what I assumed were a bunch of German cuss words. Then he spun and took off after Gregor. And I ran after Heinrich. Roosevelt and Socrates were right behind me.

But Gregor was fast.

By the time we reached the small clearing under the big tree, Gregor had already found Athena, who was tied up to the tree and barking like mad. He had bent down to untie her, his other arm wrapped around her neck. And he was talking softly into her ear. If I were a betting man, I would have put my money on the Greek alphabet.

Heinrich stopped underneath the tall California oak tree. I pulled up short behind him. Both of us were panting, but he was panting way harder.

From the waistband of his pants, he yanked out what looked like a small pistol. Swinging around, he aimed it directly at me. He was smiling, but in that evil way that bad guys do when they know they've won and they're about to tell you how you've played right into their plan.

"*Gut!* You haf played right into my plan," he said. (Called that one, didn't I?)

I swung my head around wildly, trying to make out any shapes I could. That's when I noticed that both Ed and Frank DiCarlo were tied to the base of the oak tree, their hands bound behind them, facing opposite directions.

This felt like a scene right out of a bad cowboy

movie. Except that the gun was pointed at me, and there was no rich, perfect-haired Hollywood actor coming to save my butt.

I put my hands up, palms facing Heinrich. Raising my hands above my head caused my ribs to hurt badly, but I wasn't going to let him see that if I could help it.

"Why do you want me so much?" I asked. "I just got *Pandora's Book*, like, yesterday. I don't even really know how to use it." I nodded toward Socrates. "See. Somehow I made him appear and then couldn't get him back. He's been wandering around the streets."

Heinrich turned to Ed. "You didn't tell him?"

Ed looked helpless and small under that tree. He coughed when he tried to talk. "There wasn't time," he said, through his hacks. "I thought I'd have more time."

"Tell me what!" I was getting really tired of this routine. Somebody needed to tell me *something*.

I could hear the anguish in Ed's voice when he spoke. "I'm so sorry, kid. I thought I could protect you, you know?" He hung his head and coughed a few more times.

"Protect me from what?" I looked over at Frank DiCarlo, who was watching this whole thing with interest.

"I told you to call me, didn't I, kid? I could have saved you a lot of trouble. But you didn't. You had to do it your way. I kinda like that, kid. But now you gotta figure your way outta this mess."

I looked back at Heinrich.

"Would someone please tell me what's going on?" I yelled, moving my hands now to my ribs. If he was going to shoot me, so be it. My ribs were killing me.

Heinrich kept his gun pointed at me but relaxed his arms a little. "Do you know who I am?"

"An Evil German Guy," I said. "And a dog-napper."

He cackled. But then he grew serious and looked straight at me. "My name is Heinrich Zimmerman. I served under Adolf Hitler in World War II."

"Hitler?" I gasped. "The guy who killed all the Jews?"

"Yes, zhat was him. Von of the most powerful

men of zee twentieth century," he said, with no little amount of awe in his voice.

"Hitler," I repeated. "Holy moly."

"*Ja,* holy moly," he repeated, smiling. "It is time to complete my plan. I haf both books and now I haf you." He raised his pistol.

I was starting to shiver uncontrollably, but whether it was from the cold or from fear, who knew. I figured that Socrates and Roosevelt were still behind Heinrich, but I couldn't really see them. I could barely make out the shapes of Ed and DiCarlo over by the tree. And I could hear the slurping of Athena as she lapped up every available inch of Gregor's skin behind me.

My only hope was that Roosevelt would come busting in with his gun blazing and distract Heinrich long enough that I could dive into some bushes and sneak off. I had to be ready to do that—broken rib and all.

It seemed like a good idea to keep Heinrich talking. Stall him. Isn't that what they always did in the movies when the good guy had no escape plan?

"Why did you take Athena? How can a dog possibly help your plan?" I asked.

Heinrich shrugged. "I knew you vould follow her. I zaw how much she meant to zhat boy over zhere."

Gregor was slowly pulling Athena toward the path. I truly hoped he could get them both out of this clearing and back down the mountain to safety. And fast.

"How did you get here?" I asked Heinrich. "I mean, shouldn't you be, uh, dead by now?"

Heinrich chuckled. "You'd think zo, vouldn't you? But zometimes, zhese zhings haf a vay of turning out."

This guy was nutso, bonkers, loony tunes. And he was holding a gun that was pointed toward me. I sighed. This wasn't going to end well. For some reason, I thought of Mel. Her long, lean legs. The way she'd smiled earlier and said, "You crack me up, Spencer." My heart felt heavy.

I heard some rustling in the bushes behind Heinrich. It could have been an animal scampering through the leaves or even just a breeze. But I hoped it was Roosevelt. *Please let it be Roosevelt*, I thought.

Heinrich was ramping up to tell his story and not paying attention. "Vhen Adolf Hitler died, my boy, he vas of course immortalized in zhat *Other Book*. Zhe book, at zhat time, vas being vatched over by a shopkeeper in Paris. A few years later, it made its vay to Florida, to a woman named Gigi. No one is really sure how zhis Gigi got it, only zhat zhese books haf a vay of finding the people zhey vant to find, and Gigi was next in line."

These books have a way of finding the people they want to find. Surely, they wouldn't want to find themselves in the hands of someone like this guy.

Heinrich went on. "In 1947 Al Capone had a stroke and shortly afterward, he died. Being zhe criminal mastermind zhat he vas, *Pandora's Other Book* chose to immortalize him as vell. Zhis vas a problem. Gigi had a fascination vith Al Capone. Unlike *Pandora's Book*, zhe *Other Book* comes vith clear instructions: owners are *not ever* to bring people from zheir pages to life."

Yeah, I was beginning to see why that was a good rule.

Heinrich said, "But Gigi couldn't resist. She vanted to meet zee real Al Capone. Zo she did exactly vhat she vasn't supposed to do."

Though I couldn't see him, Frank DiCarlo's voice piped up from over by the big tree. "It was supposed to be a one-time thing, see, kid. A quick meeting—badda bing, badda boom. But Gigi and I got along too well. She was a great dame. A looker, too. We had all sorts of fun, Gigi and me. She started leaving me out of the book for longer and longer periods of time. We'd go to parties together—me as Frank DiCarlo, of course. Nobody figured it out. It was a good life. Gigi was a great gal. The best."

DiCarlo seemed to be getting choked up thinking about Gigi, even after more than sixty years.

"What happened?" I asked. I had to keep these people talking and hope that Roosevelt came through for me somehow.

No one answered, and in the silence, you could literally hear crickets chirping. A breeze rustled some leaves in the tree.

DiCarlo spoke, but his tone had changed. Where

before he had sounded nostalgic, he now sounded bitter and angry. "*Pandora's Other Book* has some powerful magic, kid. You're just starting to see that. There's a balance in this world that ain't meant to be messed with—a balance between good and evil. That's what these books do, try to keep those two things in balance, you hear me? But Gigi—she was a good kid, see, but she had this thing for this *Other Book*. She wanted to see how it worked. Wanted to know what would happen. I tried to talk her out of it. But . . . but she didn't listen."

DiCarlo's voice trailed off, and when he spoke next, it was almost as if he was seeing the scene before him.

"It was the strangest thing. She just wanted to, you know, tap on a few of these guys' pictures and maybe say hi, ask a question or two, and then pop them back in the book. And for Genghis Khan—you know that Mongolian Emperor who massacred all kinds of people?—well, no problem. With Vlad the Impaler, it was, 'How do you do, what a lovely mustache and turban you have, now back in the book.' But then, we came to Adolf Hitler's page. And something crazy happened. Hitler wasn't the only guy who showed up." DiCarlo paused. "This guy here showed up, too."

For a second, I didn't know who he meant. Then it hit me. He meant Heinrich. Heinrich showed up, too.

Heinrich snorted in the darkness. "Zhere vere a few huge problems with zhat. Not only vas I not supposed to be in zee book. But . . . I vasn't dead yet."

I gasped. Holy moly.

"But . . . ? Why . . . ?" I stammered. For a second, I forgot that I was caught up in a bad climax scene of a movie and was most likely about to be captured (or killed) by this Evil Dude. All I could think was, *How could that happen?*

Heinrich's voice broke through the silence. "Zhe pictures in *Pandora's Ozher Book* vere meant to haf just zhe one person in zhem. No one else. Vhen zhey vere brought into zee present time, zhey came alone. Hitler's picture vas different. Far off in zee background, almost imperceptible to zee naked eye, vas another figure. Zhat figure vas me."

I quickly thought back to all the pictures I had seen in *Pandora's Book*. It was true. They had all been carefully cropped or taken to show only that one person being discussed on the page.

"So, vhen the Fuhrer—Hitler—vas called to Gigi's room, I vas forced to come as vell," said Heinrich. "Except zhat I vas alive and sitting in a small café in Germany at zee time, sipping an espresso and trying to figure out how to get on viz my life after zee var. You see, I vas hafing a hard time finding vork."

If he was looking for sympathy, he would have to find it in the dictionary.

DiCarlo's voice came through the darkness. "Gigi and I were stunned. For a moment, we didn't know what to do; but once we realized what had happened, we quickly tapped them both safely back into the book, and sent Heinrich back where he belonged."

I had a ton of questions. And since Roosevelt had yet to show up and save the day—was he napping? kicking back with an evening snack? hunting squirrels?—I was going to ask as many as I could.

"What happened to Gigi after that?"

DiCarlo answered, "One day, she vanished. Went out to get some cat food. Never came back. Left me with her little house in Palm Beach, her cat, and *Pandora's Other Book*. And since I couldn't put myself back in the book, I decided to become its protector. It was the perfect setup, really. I was immortal—or kind of, anyway. And I was loving life. So I was ready to fight for that book's safety no matter what."

Heinrich laughed, a hearty, evil-sounding laugh that sent willies up and down my spine. "But you had to vorry about me now didn't you, Alphonse?" Heinrich swung his attention back toward me. "In 1951 I vas in Germany vorking at a restaurant owned by my family. But I knew about zee existence of zee book now. It plagued my every vaking thought and kept me avake at night. I vasn't exactly sure how it had vorked, but I knew it vas a vay zhat I could do vhat Hitler had failed to do: achieve immortality. I knew zhere had to be all sorts of power in zhat book. If I could get my hands on it, it vould be mine."

This guy was giving me the creeps. The full-on creeps.

Frank DiCarlo interrupted. "I shoulda never gone to Germany, kid."

Heinrich cleared his throat. "But he couldn't resist. He had to see if he could find me and get rid of me himself since I was zee only von in the world who knew about zhis *Ozher Book*. I vasn't hard to find, really, vas I, Al? In fact, all you had to do vas . . ."

At that moment, Roosevelt came charging out of the darkness, hollering, "Take that, you German scoundrel!" and firing his rifle haphazardly.

I covered my head with my hands and tore off toward the tree where Ed and DiCarlo were tied. I was thinking that maybe, if I got them loose quickly enough, we could all get out of there while Roosevelt kept Heinrich busy.

Behind me, I heard the sharp *bang-bang* of Heinrich's pistol. There were some grunts and yells, but it was too dark to know if anyone was hit or hurt.

I dove for the base of the tree and slid as if I were going for home plate—feet first. My ribs howled.

"Ed," I gasped. "You okay?"

"Yeah, kid."

"Hold still. I'm going to try to set you free."

I felt around in the dirt with my hands until I found the tree and then worked my way up. Finally, my fingers looped around the ropes that were binding both Ed and DiCarlo. I was going to have to do this blindly, since it was pitch-black over here. But then, I was used to doing a lot of things in my life blindly.

"Sorry about all this," Ed said softly.

I could hear Roosevelt whooping it up in the background. I hoped he was winning.

"Yeah," I said and kept yanking at the knots. They were tied tightly. Apparently, Heinrich knew how to tie a knot.

"He's not going to win, you know," Ed said.

I said nothing. I didn't have his confidence. Heinrich had a gun and he had the books hidden somewhere. That gave him the advantage as far as I was concerned.

"He doesn't know how to work them," Ed said. "In fact, because he is *in* one of them, he can't work them. He needs one of us. Even my friend Al over there can't work the books, no matter how good his intentions might be."

Al Capone. Good intentions. Who would have thought?

One of the knots was getting looser. Just another second, and I was going to have it.

With no warning, I was knocked off my feet from behind and sent sprawling sideways into the dirt.

For a moment, I couldn't breathe. Couldn't see. Couldn't think.

Suddenly I was tired of fighting this guy, tired of thinking that I was anything but a normal sixth grader whose mom made him volunteer at an old folks' home.

So I lay there in the dirt, squeezed my eyes closed, and waited for the next blow that was sure to come.

CHAPTER 20
A LITTLE HELP
FROM MY FRIENDS

pencer!" Ed yelled gruffly. "Get up, boy! Run!"

But I couldn't. My ribs were hurting too much. I was struggling to breathe. Heinrich grabbed me roughly by the shoulder and hauled me to my feet.

"*Dumme Junge!*" Heinrich said. "You zhink I'm going to let you go, after all zhese years of plotting? Finally, zhings are coming togezher, and you zhink I'm going to give up zo easy?"

His breath was right in my ear. It smelled like sauerkraut and coffee and orange Tic Tacs.

"Spencer! Don't give in! Fight him! The books are in his knapsack, Spencer!" Ed yelled. "It's up to you, boy. That's why you were chosen. To fight."

Everything on my body hurt. I was cold. Hungry. Tired. I wanted nothing more than to be in my room doing math homework with Gregor. The book hadn't chosen me; I was sure of it. Ed was an old, senile guy who'd handed it off to a nice kid because I'd taken him out to the railroad tracks every day. That was all.

"I just want to go home," I whispered.

"And go home you shall," Heinrich said reassuringly. "Vonce you've made the books vork, my young *freund.*"

He was pushing me toward the path, away from Ed and Al, in the direction that Gregor and Athena had gone earlier. I hoped they were long gone, far down this mountain, close to help by now. I scanned the dark, trying to see, but my eyes are useless at night. I nearly tripped on something on the ground before me and then realized it was Roosevelt, moaning and clearly wounded.

"Colonel Roosevelt!" I said. "Are you okay?"

He moaned again and muttered, "Attack, men, up and over the hill. Don't stop until they've surrendered."

I hoped that meant he would live long enough for us to get him safely back into *Pandora's Book*. If we could get *Pandora's Book* back from Heinrich.

"Where are we going?" I asked as we hurtled down the path, him pushing me from behind, me trying to keep my footing in the nearly pitch-blackness.

"Just move!"

I nearly tripped several times. Once, I lost my balance completely and went down on a knee. I cried out in pain, but Heinrich simply yanked me back up and kept pushing me along. Wherever we were headed, he wanted us to get there fast.

I was at least encouraged that we were going toward civilization. I figured that maybe I could cry out for help, or someone might notice an odd-looking, gun-wielding guy and a shivering kid in running clothes hustling along the sidewalk.

But then, about halfway down the trail, Heinrich yanked me to the left abruptly. Soon we were traipsing through brush and bushes. Branches cut at my bare legs, and grasses rubbed against me, making me instantly itchy. All sorts of creepy-crawly things—rattlesnakes and scorpions and who knew what else—lived in these hills. One bite from them, and I'd be a goner. But I guess I had bigger problems than a rattlesnake bite at the moment.

Heinrich was shoving me farther and farther into the brush. My face and arms were getting torn up by sharp branches that I couldn't see to push away before they tore at my skin. Twice my glasses were ripped off my face, and I had to grab at them before they were swept into the darkness and trampled or lost forever.

At times we headed up the mountain, and I could feel the land slope upward beneath my feet. My breathing would become labored—as would Heinrich's—and we would trudge more slowly. Then abruptly we'd change directions, sliding downhill for several hundred yards, my calves and shins burning as the ground fell away beneath me.

My fear melted into exhaustion, which morphed into anger. Again and again, I cycled through every emotion possible. As the minutes wore on, I lost track of time and any sense of direction. I could only march on at Heinrich's insistence, hoping that at some point he would use me for whatever task he needed and then let me go. Somehow, though, I didn't think he would—let me go, anyway.

Finally, I felt the land level out. In the faint moonlight, I saw that we had reached the crest of the mountain we'd been climbing. There was no trail up here, just a wide expanse of tall grasses, some small shrubs, and the occasional oak tree. I had a general idea of where we were, since I could see the twinkling lights of Rio Valle below us. We'd climbed to the ridge of one of the mountains bordering the town where I lived. No wonder I was wiped out.

Heinrich released me, but stayed close. Immediately, I collapsed to the ground. I hugged my legs gently and folded forward to cradle my sore ribs.

"What do you want me to do?" I asked tiredly. "Can we just do it and be done?"

"Patience, *mein sohn*," Heinrich said.

He lifted his knapsack off his shoulder, and set it gently on the ground. I saw his gun glinting in the moonlight from the waistband of his pants.

Carefully, he opened the flap and pulled out *Pandora's Book*. He handed it to me. Then he pulled out *Pandora's Other Book* and hugged it to his chest.

I was close enough and there was enough moonlight to barely see his face. And Heinrich, at this moment, looked how I imagined a father might look when he first held his newborn son.

"Vhen I learned about the existence of zhese books, I zhought only about how it might make me immortal," he said. "If it could bring Adolf back from the dead, it could do zhee same for me."

"And that's what the world needs—two madmen brought back from the dead," I said, looking down at my running shoes.

Heinrich acted as if he hadn't heard me. "But zhen I realized zhere vas so much more zhat could be done wizh zhese books. In zhem, zhe greatest minds of zee vorld are stored forever. Just zhink, Spencer, if zhey vere all brought back and used for the single purpose of creating a stronger and more powerful human race . . . Can you imagine zee possibilities?"

I stared up at Heinrich. Maybe he and Hitler had

even more in common than I'd thought. A stronger and more powerful human race? Was he nuts?

"I know it sounds crazy," Heinrich said, his voice low and controlled. He could hardly contain his excitement. "But listen to me. . . . You and I are going to open Pandora's box for real, Spencer. Ve're going to bring togezher all zee good and evil zhat zee vorld has ever had to offer, all zee best minds of history, and ve are going to harness zheir visdom, zheir talents, zheir power to create zee most advanced society ever. And zee best part? I'm immortal, *mein sohn*! Being from zhat book has allowed me to live vithout getting any older! Vith your help, I can create zee strongest, most advanced culture and rule it forever!"

That's when I knew. I had to stop him. No matter how much my ribs hurt. No matter how little I had left in my fighting arsenal. No matter how weak and underprepared I was for this battle, I had to try. And if I died doing it, then at least he'd have no way to access the people in these books.

I stumbled to my feet.

"I won't help you," I said, clutching *Pandora's Book* to my chest.

He reached into the waistband of his pants and removed his gun. He pulled it out and held it so it pointed right at my chest. Heinrich laughed. "You haf no choice."

There was a snap in the bushes to our left.

"There is always a choice."

Heinrich and I both swung our heads toward the voice at the same time to see Socrates climbing up over the crest of the hill. *"He who is not contented with what he has, would not be contented with what he would like to have."*

Heinrich turned his gun on Socrates. "Stand back, old man! I don't need your silly platitudes."

"Let him who would move the world first move himself," Socrates said calmly, continuing to walk toward Heinrich.

"Halt!" Heinrich screamed. "I mean it! Stop!" He was waving his gun wildly. Something about Socrates's slow advancement was clearly freaking him out.

Heinrich fired off a shot, but since he was still

holding *Pandora's Other Book* in one hand, it missed Socrates by a mile. Socrates blinked and kept moving forward, one slow step at a time.

Just then, the outline of another person popped over the edge of the ridge. A dog bounded next to him, nipping playfully at his heels. Gregor. And Athena.

"Gregor! No!" I shouted. "Turn around! Go back down! Get help, okay?"

But Gregor kept walking toward me. My eyesight was too cruddy, but I was willing to bet my favorite running shoes that the hand not holding Athena's leash was tapping a mile a minute on his thighs.

"Nineteen seventy-two," he said, his voice quavering but still audible in the quiet night air. "*Mariner 9* sends pictures from Mars. The Easter Offensive begins after North Vietnamese soldiers cross into the DMZ of South Vietnam. Richard Nixon and Russian President Brezhnev sign the SALT I treaty in Moscow...."

Oh, dear God, I prayed silently. *Make him stop. Turn him around. He's going to get us all killed.*

"Gregor," I pleaded, my voice strained.

Gregor kept walking. So did Socrates.

And then another person showed up. This one much older and limping.

"Details," Ed said gruffly. His body was racked by a fit of coughing so hard that he had to pause and bend at the waist. "What is life without all the details, Spencer?"

Heinrich was pointing his gun again, this time at Gregor and Athena. But his aim was still off, and the bullet flew harmlessly into the cool night air.

"You can't stop me!" Heinrich yelled. "Power is on my side now! I haf zee books."

The books. It was as if a lightbulb exploded inside my head. I knew instantly what to do. But I had to do it quickly. Because once Heinrich figured it out, he'd do anything to try to stop me.

His attention was still on the three people advancing almost zombielike toward us. As silently as possible, I flipped open *Pandora's Book*. I wasn't exactly sure who I was looking for, but it was as if *Pandora's Book* knew better than I did. The pages fell open easily to

President John F. Kennedy. Quickly, I grabbed the bookmark from its spot in the back and prayed that I would do this correctly. I slid the white cardboard rectangle from the spine outward across JFK's picture and then tapped quickly—thumb to pinky and back again—on his page. In seconds, he stood next to me on the hilltop.

"A man may die, nations may rise and fall, but an idea lives on," our thirty-fifth President said in his clipped Boston accent. I wanted to hug him.

Heinrich swung around.

"Vhat?" he asked, startled. "Vhat are you doing?"

I grabbed a hunk of pages and flipped ahead.

Martin Luther King Jr. Perfect.

"An individual has not started living until he can rise above the narrow confines of his individualistic concerns to the broader concerns of all humanity," he said, his preacher's voice rising up for the entire city to hear.

"Vords von't stop me, Spencer," Heinrich said. "I've vaited too long."

I flipped ahead in *Pandora's Book*. He was right. Words wouldn't stop him. We needed some firepower.

I squinted at the picture open before me. I smiled down at *Pandora's Book*. It knew.

"Nice," I whispered.

General Stonewall Jackson looked a lot more, I don't know, ordinary, I guess, than I expected him to be. I somehow figured that a guy who kicked that much butt fighting for the Confederate army during the Civil War should have been, like, really ripped. He was actually kind of skinny.

General Jackson immediately turned to me. Even my sucky vision was able to make out his intense blue eyes. "You need help, young man?"

I nodded. "That guy over there with the gun and the book. We need to get the book from him before he hurts anyone."

Stonewall Jackson fingered his bushy brown beard once before reaching down and withdrawing a pistol with a long, thin barrel from a holster near his hip. "One man shouldn't be too difficult to manage after facing that gutless General McClellan's troops at Antietam."

It would have been better if he'd been on a horse—

more dramatic, probably—but the way Stonewall charged Heinrich with his pistol raised was really sweet. It was as if the man had been doing it all his life. If it didn't hurt so dang much, I would have raised a fist to cheer him on.

But just as Stonewall was within firing range, Heinrich spun and sent off a shot of his own. It clipped Stonewall on the shoulder. Stonewall faltered, though amazingly he didn't stop charging and managed to fire his long-barreled gun. Then the weapon fell from his hands, and he clutched his shoulder in pain. It was only seconds before a growing stain of blood came seeping through Stonewall's shirt.

Heinrich, too, had taken a bullet from Stonewall's well-aimed shot. He had one hand firmly pressed against his hip and was limping backward, toward the opposite side of the mountain. His other hand still clung to *Pandora's Other Book.*

I ran toward Stonewall, who stood where he'd been shot, looking dazed.

"General Jackson?" More blood was oozing from

his shoulder. Stonewall looked up at me with glassy eyes. "Are you okay?"

Stonewall smiled, a smile full of wisdom and pain and resolve. "Listen to me, son. You got to get him running, you hear? Once you get him running, you stay right on top of him. It's how a smaller guy can defeat a larger guy, you hear me? *Only thus can a weaker country cope with a stronger; it must make up in activity what it lacks in strength.*"

I knew I needed to get the general back in *Pandora's Book*, where I was pretty sure he would be good as new, healed from today's wounds. I flipped open to his page—now blank—and called out to Ed, "Help me, Ed! I've got to get him back! How do I do this?"

Ed coughed twice—so hard, I was worried he was going to spew up body parts—and said, "Just reverse it, Spencer—what you did to get him here—and end by dragging the fingernail of your index finger across the page."

I did exactly as he said and breathed a sigh as Stonewall vanished from the ground before me and showed up safely on the page of *Pandora's Book*.

Quickly, I did the same for Socrates, President Kennedy, and Martin Luther King Jr. They had been good distractions. But it was time to take on this guy myself.

I looked up quickly and spotted Heinrich near the far side of the hill. He was little more than a dark outline now, still backing away from all of us. I knew he must be holding that vicious little gun of his, since I had yet to see him drop it. And of course, he had *Pandora's Other Book*.

Gregor was by my side. Athena reached over to give my hand a good lick. Absently, I patted her head.

"What do we do, G.?" I asked quietly. "He's going to get away if we don't stop him now. And I need that other book. We have to get him back into it."

"In 1863 General Stonewall Jackson fought the Battle of Chancellorsville against General Joseph Hooker of the Union Army," Gregor recited softly, not meeting my eyes.

I felt a surge of frustration. "Gregor, seriously, I need your help."

"Hooker's army was twice the size of the Confederate army. But the Battle of Chancellorsville is often considered one of the Confederate army's most perfect battles because they made the risky decision to divide their forces even though they were up against a larger enemy army."

"Gregor, I . . . ," I started and stopped.

The frustration drained out of me. Gregor *was* helping me. He was telling me exactly what to do. They'd all been telling me what to do—Kennedy, MLK Jr., Stonewall Jackson, and even Ed and Socrates. In their own ways, they'd been telling me all along.

I closed my eyes, and when I opened them, Gregor was looking at me expectantly.

"We can outrun him, buddy," I said.

He nodded.

Ed had been making his way slowly toward us. Finally, he was close enough that I could hand him *Pandora's Book*.

"I'm going to give this back to you for a little while," I said grimly. "Take good care of it."

Ed nodded. "I'm gonna go put Teddy Roosevelt

back in these pages where he belongs. I hope to be enjoying some pork chops and French Onion Soup when you get back."

That sounded so good. I hoped he'd save some for us. I hoped there'd be an *us* to save some for.

The grin faded from Ed's face. "Spencer," he said, his voice completely void of its usual jokiness, "did Mel ever find you?"

I looked away. In all that had happened during the last hour or so, I'd forgotten about Mel. "She found us, Ed," I said. "She was awesome. But Heinrich . . . at the senior center . . . he hurt her, Ed. She was taken to the hospital."

I saw Ed look off into the distance and stare for a moment at the lights below. Somewhere down there in that city, doctors were working on his granddaughter.

"I was trying to protect her, Spencer. Her parents are . . . well, they would not be the best people to know about this book. It's why . . . it's why I didn't tell you about her. . . . But I don't know. Maybe it would have saved you both."

"Don't, Ed," I said softly. "Mel's tough. She's a fighter."

He nodded, and then turned back to me. "Be careful, Spencer," he said. "He's a really bad guy. But you can do this. You have to."

Gregor handed Athena's leash to Ed. I took one last look at Ed and *Pandora's Book*. Thought about how crazy my life had become in just a few short days.

And then I thought about the guy who was ready to resurrect Joseph Stalin—a Soviet leader who had killed hundreds of thousands of Russians. Attila the Hun. Adolf Hitler. The most hated and despised people in history. Even if he couldn't get me to work *Pandora's Other Book* for him, eventually he'd find someone who would. I had to stop him. Now.

I looked at Gregor. "Ready, Pheidippides?"

He nodded solemnly. "I'm as ready as you are, Koroibos."

And we took off.

CHAPTER 21
WE SAVE THE WORLD
(MOSTLY)

Heinrich wasn't hard to follow. He was staggering at this point, loudly snapping through branches and brush. Plus, he was howling in pain. Apparently, our Evil German Guy was kind of a wimp.

We caught up to him fairly easily. Even though A) my ribs hurt crazy bad, B) I was insanely cold and tired, and C) we hadn't eaten since our tiny little lunch half a lifetime ago—both Gregor and I had a renewed energy to go kick this guy's butt, get him back in *Pandora's Other Book*, and end this horrible night.

Heinrich didn't even seem to notice we were following him. So it was easy to stay a safe distance behind him as he stumbled down the mountain-side. While we walked, we tried to formulate a plan.

"I think we should come at him from different sides," I said. "I'll grab the book, and you kick the gun away."

"I don't want to do the gun, Spencer," Gregor said nervously. "And I don't kick very well."

He had a point. We'd done a karate unit in PE. And Gregor had made it look more like ballet.

"Okay, how about this?" I whispered. "You stay about ten feet away and make some loud noises to distract him, while I run in and grab the book from his arms."

"What if he shoots at me?" Gregor asked, his eyes wide, his fingers tapping.

I threw up my hands. "Come on, dude! Work with me here." Maybe I should have come alone. "What do you want to do, then, G.?"

Gregor was quiet for a minute. "How about I run up from behind and cover his eyes and you run at him from the side and grab the book?"

Seriously? *This* was his brilliant plan? It sounded like something Anthony "The Gut" Gutterson would do—no, had done—to us on the playground many times. But if Gregor was willing (especially since it required Gregor to touch the guy, and you know how Gregor feels about touching), then I was game.

"Okay," I said, taking a deep breath. "You ready to do this? On three?"

Gregor was tapping as fast as I've ever seen him tap, but he nodded.

I'm going to stop here for a minute—not for long, because I know you're itching to see how our brilliant plan of attack worked out. Before we get into that, though, I want you to know this: we really thought this might work. I know it sounds lame now as you read this. But while we stood on that mountaintop, we had all the hope in the world that we could get the job done easily and go home.

Heinrich was about a hundred yards from us, still staggering in a zigzag pattern down the mountain. I had to believe that he didn't know where he was going at that moment, or maybe he was hurting too much to think straight. Because he certainly wasn't walking straight. He was still hollering like mad, too.

"One," I whispered, and Gregor and I got into our runners' crouches. "Two." We both held our breaths. "Three." We took off.

Gregor shot straight down toward Heinrich—a whirring dart of speed and agility. I veered off to the left so I could make a wide arc and come at Heinrich from the side. I had to run as fast as I could since I was running a longer distance, and I don't have to tell you that Gregor is naturally faster.

Gregor reached Heinrich seconds before I did. For a nanosecond, he hesitated and I could imagine his repulsion. But then he reached up and threw his arms around Heinrich's head, putting Heinrich in a kind of headlock and blocking his eyesight.

Heinrich immediately cried out and started struggling.

I had only seconds to grab *Pandora's Other Book* and get the heck out of there.

I was two steps away when Heinrich dropped the book to the ground and reached for his gun, which he'd shoved back into the waistband of his pants.

I heard the thud of the book and saw Gregor and Heinrich scuffle.

There was a flash of metal in the moonlight as Heinrich pulled out the gun. It took a second before my brain registered what was about to happen.

"NO!" I screamed and lunged for both of them, forgetting about the book, thinking only about my best friend.

There was a loud explosion as the gun went off, and both Heinrich and Gregor fell to the ground, me on top of them. I felt another crack in my ribs, a splinter of pain that shot up, up, up into my heart and jaw and skull; but all my brain could process was *Gregor—gun—Gregor—gun.*

There was a tangle of limbs and grunts as we scuffled there on the ground—all three of us—me not knowing who was moving and who wasn't, only that I needed to roll off, roll aside, and get to Gregor.

Finally I managed to free myself from the mess. I rolled to my side—my good side. I could see Gregor, but he was facedown in the dirt and weeds. Heinrich lay partially on top of him, not moving.

"Gregor?" I reached for his shoulder and poked him. "Gregor! Say something."

Everything had gone painfully, eerily quiet.

Please God. My body felt numb, light.

My fault. So my fault.

Please. God.

Then Gregor moaned. He didn't move. But that low moan let me know he was alive, and a rush of relief exploded in me. I managed somehow to sit up and scooch closer to my friend.

My best friend.

I heaved with all my strength to push Heinrich off of him, noting that Heinrich was as limp as a rag doll. I grabbed Gregor by both shoulders and shook him gently. There was no blood that I could see, but it was dark, too dark to tell much. My eyes were horrible. Even straining, I could only see shapes.

"Gregor," I pleaded. "Talk to me. Please."

The tears were coming, rushing down my cheeks, and I didn't care. I needed him to be okay. He'd stayed by my side this whole day. He'd fought his fear, the impulses of his body that made even the smallest acts of everyday life hard, to be with me. I would not leave him. And I would not let him leave me.

Carefully, I rolled him over, making sure that I wasn't hurting him. He was breathing—I could see his chest rising and falling. But his eyes were closed. Once he was on his back, I could see it. Where the bullet had hit. A large dark circle on his stomach, just to the left of his belly button.

"Oh, God! Gregor!" I cried. "Help!" My voice rang out in the stillness. Would Ed hear? "Help us!"

Panic was quickly taking over my body; I felt nothing except its monstrous claws wrapping around my heart. He had to live. He had to. Or it would be my fault.

And I needed him.

Something brushed my leg. Heinrich was stirring. Moaning. His legs moving.

I had another problem now.

Pandora's Other Book lay only a few feet away, having landed open where Heinrich had dropped it, some pages smashed into the ground, its heavy spine crushing them.

I crawled toward the book, my tears making dark little circles on the ground. I would rid the world of this monster. Right now.

I flipped the book over. I didn't know what page he was on, but *Pandora's Other Book* did, and it showed me the way.

Page 134. For some reason, that number seemed like it should mean something. But my mind was coming up with nothing, and I didn't have time to figure it out now.

The page wasn't blank like most pages. There was a black-and-white image of Hitler in uniform, saluting, his arm and fingers straight out. But in the very upper left corner, there was a blank spot. As if someone had been cropped out of the photo. And indeed, someone had.

But he was about to be popped back in.

I found the bookmark in the back. I slid it as Ed had showed me, but in reverse and then tapped my fingers like I had for Stonewall. Finally, with one last glance at Heinrich, who was now waking up, I held my forefinger over the image, ready to swipe it.

Heinrich's eyes opened enough for him to see what I was about to do.

"Spencer, *mein sohn*," he said groggily. "Ve could do zhis togezher. Zo much power. You and me."

I stared at him, feeling more loathing for him than I had ever felt for another person. But there was another feeling, too. Pity.

"You don't even belong in this book, Heinrich," I said. And then I swiped my fingernail across the page.

And he was gone.

I looked down at the open page of the book. There he was, a grainy figure in the far background of Hitler's photo. An afterthought. Not even worth a passing glance.

Decisively, I closed the book and tossed it aside.

I crawled back to my friend.

Gregor needed help, and he needed it quickly. But we were on top of a mountain. And my cell phone was still missing somewhere. Ed wasn't strong enough to make the hike over here.

I had to think.

Gregor's chest was rising and falling, but more and more blood was seeping out of his wound. I took off my shirt and pressed it into his side, hoping I could at least slow the flow.

I looked up into the moonlit sky.

Please, God. I know it's a lot to ask. But I need help on this. Give me a sign of what I should do. Please?

I closed my eyes and gently pushed my hands into Gregor's stomach. And continued to pray.

CHAPTER 22

BY THE NUMBERS

The minutes were passing slowly. Several times, I wondered if I should go find help, but I knew I couldn't leave Gregor there. So I waited. And prayed. And shivered. And prayed some more.

He moaned every so often and I'd think he was about to wake up and tell me he was okay. But then he wouldn't. Once he even opened his eyes. I knew he couldn't see me, though. And that was even creepier than if he'd kept them closed.

I wondered if there was anyone in *Pandora's Other Book* who could help us. But those people were all the monsters of the past. The people who killed others.

Not the people who cured or healed or helped; they were in *Pandora's Book*.

I wondered how Mel was doing. I thought about my parents. My sister. They were probably frantic with worry. I hoped they had sent out a search party. But if they had, I doubted the search party would find its way up here.

I wondered if maybe Athena had some Lassie capabilities in her. Maybe she was pulling at Ed, trying to tell him that Gregor was in trouble. But even if she was, would Ed have a clue? Probably not. I could just picture him telling her war stories. Or maybe he'd conjured up that one chef lady from *Pandora's Book*, and she was making them all chocolate chip cookies. My stomach rumbled.

Mostly, though, I thought about Gregor. What a great friend he was. How he never let me down, even when he was being his most crazy, weird Gregor. And then I would cry a little bit. And then I would tell myself to quit being such a baby. And then the whole cycle would start again.

After what seemed like forever, I heard some

really loud movements in the bushes. I froze. Gregor and I were sitting ducks out here for coyotes, mountain lions, or anything else that might have smelled his blood and been hungry. My heart started hammering. I'd fought off Heinrich. But a starving mountain lion?

It wasn't an animal, though. It was a human.

"Hey!" I yelled. "I need help!"

It was too dark to tell who it was or even if it was male or female. The figure was small. It wore a hooded jacket. It walked timidly, with small footsteps, and was hunched over. And it didn't call back to me.

"Please!" I called again. "My friend is hurt!"

The person was coming closer but was in no hurry, taking his or her time and stopping every few steps to peek up at me from under the hood that shadowed his or her face.

I was getting nervous again. Maybe this wasn't help. There were a lot of weirdos out here. It suddenly occurred to me that someone roaming around the mountains at night might not be a friend.

The person was getting closer now, but still had not said a word. I could see a long dark coat with a sweatshirt underneath. The hood of the sweatshirt was pulled up. Big, heavy boots. Definitely not the kind of clothes you'd wear if you were going hiking.

Yet there was something oddly familiar about this person.

He or she kept coming closer, but so, so tentatively, almost as if they were afraid of me, not the other way around. I held my breath. Just steps away now.

"Please," I said quietly. "We need help."

The person said nothing. He or she walked closer still. Right up to me. Stood above me. The person was not tall, but with Gregor and me on the ground, helpless, they had the clear advantage. My body quivered involuntarily.

With a gloved hand, the person reached into the front pocket of the heavy coat. I swallowed and felt my stomach clench. After all we'd been through, I couldn't believe it would end like this.

But it wasn't a gun or a knife. With careful slowness, the gloved hand reached out and handed me a cell phone—an old, beat-up one. That's when I looked up and saw who was under that hood.

Phylis.

"Seven hundred fifty-six steps," she mumbled. "Call 9-1-1 for help. Or 555-8244 for the police. An ambulance is 555-7733. But I would call 9-1-1."

Tears sprang to my eyes, and a bubble of laughter rose up. I wanted to hug her, but I needed to get my friend some help first.

I took the phone from Phylis.

"Thank you, Phylis," I said. "You just made two new friends tonight."

As I punched in the three numbers that would eventually get us out of here, I suddenly knew where I'd seen the page number for Heinrich. Page 134. The grandfather clock in Ed's room. It was stopped at that time. Ed had been trying to tell us all along.

"Nine-one-one emergency," said the calm voice on the line. "How can I help you?"

I looked down at Gregor.

"My best friend," I said, feeling my throat close. "He's been shot."

CHAPTER 23
GETTING BACK TO NORMAL (KIND OF)

The bullet had only grazed Gregor's skin, so the wound looked much worse than it was. After I called for help, a helicopter landed on the mountain just steps away from where Gregor and I were waiting. If I hadn't been totally freezing and sure that my best friend was dying, it would have been the coolest thing that ever happened to me. He and I were both loaded into that emergency helicopter and airlifted off the mountain.

Phylis, by that time, had scurried off into the darkness.

It was a short ride to the hospital, but with a warm blanket around my shoulders and paramedics working on my friend and reassuring me that he was going to be fine, I finally had a moment to close my eyes and relax. I was gripping *Pandora's Other Book*—that was my job from now on, I supposed—to protect it no matter what. But I guess I had proven I was capable of that job.

There was a commotion when we landed, medical personnel rushing out to wheel Gregor off the helicopter and into the hospital—and quickly into surgery, where they would stitch him up and call him good as new. I was put in a wheelchair and a cute nurse fussed over me the whole way into the hospital. Inside I was greeted by a swarm of people who checked my vitals, asked me a bunch of stupid questions like, "Does anything hurt?" (yeah, like everything), and then wheeled me into the ER, where some X-rays were ordered.

About that time, my family arrived. (Sigh.)

I had figured out during the helicopter ride that I needed to put together a version of this story that somehow combined as much truth as possible with a few big-time omissions. Unless I wanted to be seeing a school psychologist (or worse) for the rest of my junior high school career, I was going to have to lie a little. Something I'm not generally very good at.

"Spencer!" My mom burst into tears when she saw me lying in the bed of the small ER room. I had no idea how I looked at that point, but I'd done battle with quite a few twigs and branches, gone toe-to-toe with an Evil German Guy, probably broken at least one rib, and watched two of my friends (if you could call Mel a friend) get taken out by said Evil German Guy. So yeah, I probably looked terrible.

My dad seemed very uncomfortable. He hung around the door, told me he was glad I was okay, and eventually said he was going to check out the cafeteria and he'd be back. I guessed they'd left my sister somewhere else or she'd have been crawling all over me by now, asking four million questions.

My mom sat on the edge of my bed and brushed my hair off my face.

"Oh, Spencer," she said quietly. "We were so worried when you and Gregor didn't turn up for dinner, and nobody knew where you were."

"I'm really, really sorry about that, Mom," I said sincerely.

"You want to tell me what happened? Gregor's mom is near hysterical, as you can imagine."

I thought about Mrs. Chandramouli and what she must have gone through during the past few hours.

I decided it was probably best to figure out what my mom knew and build off that.

"When did you know something was wrong? I mean, that we weren't coming home?" I asked my mom.

"Well," she said, taking a deep breath. "I got home from my yoga class and you guys obviously weren't there; but some of your school stuff was so I knew you'd been home. Plus, you left the back door unlocked, even though we've talked about that a hundred times, Spencer."

I inwardly rolled my eyes. If she only knew that we'd bolted after a guy who'd possibly kidnapped Mel and Gregor's dog at that point, she wouldn't have been so concerned about the stupid back door.

"But I figured maybe you'd gone to Gregor's house

to grab something. Then it got to be dinnertime and you still didn't show up, and I started to worry a little. When Mrs. Chandramouli called a little later to say that Athena was missing, and did you boys have her over at our house, I got *really* worried. I called the coach to see if you had been to practice, which I guess you had been. So then nothing seemed to make sense. When your dad got home, I told him to get in the car and start driving around to see if he could find you. Meanwhile, I was trying to call your cell phone— which went to *voice mail*, by the way." Mom glared at me meaningfully. "And I also tried calling anyone I could think of who might know where you were. Finally I called the Everlasting Home for Seniors as a last-ditch effort and found out that Ed was missing."

I had to applaud my mom's detective work. She wasn't half bad.

"I started thinking about that guy who'd showed up at our door the day before and how'd he'd seemed kind of weird and how he'd known you. And then the lady at Everlasting explained how they'd had an incident with a guy pulling a gun and firing at Ed's room when she'd thought you and Gregor were in there, but then you guys had vanished. Things started sounding really fishy. And dangerous. So we called the police."

She gave me her Mom look then. The one where she is trying to see inside my brain and figure out how I could possibly be her son.

I looked away and cleared my throat.

"We didn't mean for this to happen, Mom," I said. And then I launched into an abbreviated version of the afternoon—minus the dead people coming back to life; minus the Evil German Guy who was a Nazi; and minus the fact that I was now the chosen guardian of at least one super big-deal book that held a lot of killer mojo power.

Basically, I told her that we went back to get Athena, decided to go see Ed, stumbled upon his kidnapper, who dragged us to the top of our local mountains; we tried to escape; Gregor got shot; the kidnapper got away; end of story.

Yeah, it didn't sound all that believable to me either. But she bought it.

"You're going to have to talk to the police, Spencer," she said, smoothing the sheets covering my legs.

Great, I thought. Pretty sure lying to the cops was some kind of federal offense. But then, telling them the truth was bound to land me in far deeper trouble.

My mom swallowed and looked down. "I'm glad you're okay," she said quietly.

"Me, too," I said.

She leaned in to hug me, and it was the nicest hug I'd gotten in a long, long time.

I stayed that night in the hospital so they could treat me for a few broken ribs and some mild hypothermia. Gregor came out of surgery fine, and by the next morning, I was able to go see him. He was groggy but awake.

"Hey, G.," I said when I padded into his room. I was being released in an hour or two, but Gregor had to stay another day so they could make sure his wound didn't get infected. His mom was thrilled with that idea since she'd threatened to lock him up for a few weeks when he got out anyway.

"Hi, Spencer," Gregor said slowly, but it sounded like he had cotton balls in his mouth.

I pulled a chair up really close to his bed and leaned in.

"I'm so sorry about what happened to you."

"It's okay, Spencer," he said. "It was my plan."

I smiled. "It was a crazy plan. But it worked, kind of. We got Heinrich back in the book."

Gregor smiled weakly. "He wasn't a nice guy."

"Yeah, no doubt," I said. I took a breath. "Hey, Gregor, listen. A lot of people are going to ask you questions about what happened. You can't tell them about the books, okay? Or about what really happened. You have to just say that we were, you know, trying to help Ed out." I told him all the details I'd given my mom.

Gregor didn't say anything for a minute, and my stomach dropped. Gregor didn't like lying. And he sucked at it.

"I think, Spencer," he said, slowly. I held my breath. "That this will be our secret."

I exhaled. "Yes. Our secret."

He turned his head slightly toward me. "But Spencer?"

"Yeah, man?" I asked, standing up.

"We can still use *Pandora's Book*, right? Like we did with Socrates? If we promise not to lose anybody?"

I grinned. "Absolutely, G."

He closed his eyes, and I knew it was time to tip-toe out.

I had one more stop to make before I went back to my room to check out.

I'd found out her room number from one of the nurses. (Who, by the way, had a hard time holding back a grin. I guess she thought she was playing cupid or something. *Ew.*)

Mel was sitting up in bed when I came in. Ed was in the chair next to her. Her whole head was wrapped in a large bandage.

"Nicely done, runner boy," she said when she saw

me and grinned. "I wasn't sure you'd get the job done, but that was not bad."

My heart did this little flip-flop seeing her again. Even though her head was bandaged and what remained showing of her face was all black and blue, she was very, very cute.

"Thanks for the vote of confidence, Mel," I said. "Hey, Ed."

I nodded in his direction.

Ed grinned widely. "How you feeling today?"

"Like I've been run over by a school bus. Other than that, great."

"You did it, though, kid. Good triumphs over evil and all that hoopla."

I chuckled, but it hurt my ribs. "Yeah."

"I've got something for you, kid."

He pushed himself out of his chair slowly, every joint looking like it had to hurt, and took a few pain-ful-looking steps over to a worn backpack on the table. From it, he pulled out *Pandora's Book*.

"It's yours now, Spence," he said, handing it to

me. "For good. Just bring it by once in a while, will ya? So I can get some pork chops and French Onion Soup."

"No prob," I said. I tucked it under my arm.

"How about *Pandora's Other Book*?" It was still in my hospital room, hidden under my stinky clothes from yesterday. I was actually nervous about leaving it there. But then, I was nervous about having it in my possession, also. "Do I keep that, too?"

"I think we'll give that one back to DiCarlo, eh?" he said with a wink. "He's been taking good care of it for half a century now. We'll let him deal with it a little bit longer. But you two need to stay in touch, okay? You need to make sure those books are always in your care."

I was pretty happy about the thought of turning that other book over to DiCarlo. It still gave me the creeps. Kind of funny when you thought about it, though; I was entrusting the world's most dangerous and valuable book to the notorious gangster Al Capone. Who would've thought?

Ed grabbed his backpack and flung it on his

shoulders. He turned and gave Mel a little salute and then spun around to wink at me.

"I'll leave you two to chat a bit, eh?"

And then he hobbled out of the room, whistling and humming something about being in love again. Mel looked at me and rolled her eyes.

After Ed left, Mel fingered the edge of her sheet while I gazed out the hospital window and tried desperately to think of something to say that wasn't totally dumb. The silence grew painful.

"So," I said finally, "you're okay."

"Yeah," she scoffed. "It was just a bruise. I don't even know why I'm still in here."

"So, you, uh, talk to your parents?" I sat in the chair Ed had just left.

Mel looked down at her hands. Suddenly, I noticed they were clenched into fists.

"Nah. They're busy."

"Too busy to call and see if you're okay?" The words were out before I could take them back. I winced.

Mel shrugged. "Not the first time."

"Where do you live?" I asked. I was intensely curious about this girl—who was obviously so bright, so athletic, and so strong-willed. Not to mention beautiful.

She snorted. "The house where my parents live is in San Diego. They sent me up here to go to school. They wanted me to be close to Ed."

"You'll go back to school then? When you're released from here?" I asked.

"Probably." She shrugged again. "Unless they have our housekeeper or somebody come spend a few days with me at home. I don't know. Depends on when they fly in from Cairo or wherever they are."

Wow. So Mel's family *did* have a lot of money. But that was weird, because she and Ed seemed so . . . well . . . normal.

"So, anyway," she said, brightening and pasting a smile on her face. The room instantly warmed, along with my insides. "Tell me what happened after I got clocked by that idiot."

So I leaned back and filled her in on all the details. Well, maybe I exaggerated one or two—you know, to make things sounds more exciting, or um, heroic. But mostly, I kept to the true story. Seriously, I did.

After about a half an hour, I glanced up at the clock on the wall and realized that my parents would be there soon to pick me up.

Looking at the clock, though, reminded me of the one last question I had.

"I've wanted to ask you," I said, fingering the edge of the sling on my arm. "What was written on the clock in Ed's room? The grandfather clock?"

Mel's eyes slid down and her fingers starting twisting her sheets.

"It's not really important," she said.

But I looked closely and saw a faint blush of color stain her cheeks. I had every intention of checking out that grandfather clock as soon as I got back to the Everlasting Home for Seniors. Count on it.

"So, um," I said suddenly, feeling as if there were a wad of gum stuck in my throat. "Will I get to, you know, hang out with you again? When we're *not* getting shot at by bad guys?"

Mel smiled and maybe even looked kind of shy herself. "That'd be cool." She pointed to a cell phone on the table. "You got your cell phone? Let's exchange numbers. You can text me."

And that's how I got my first phone number from a girl. In a hospital room after an epic battle with an evil guy who tried to take over the world. Cool, huh?

I won't say things went back to normal after that, because that would be a lie. But we didn't have evil guys chasing us anymore so in that sense, things were, well, at least calm.

Gregor came in third at the track finals a few weeks later despite having a bandage around his entire midsection. His mother didn't want him to run, but Coach and Gregor wore her down, especially after the doctor gave the okay. My friend is amazing.

I sat out and cheered—still nursing two broken ribs. I didn't mind a bit, because Mel was in the stands next to me. And when Gregor crossed the finish line, she turned and flung her arms around me.

It hurt my ribs like everything when she hugged me. But it was so worth it.

Gregor and I figured out that if we got our homework done quickly, we could experiment with *Pandora's Book*. Our favorites were Socrates (of course); Ben Franklin (he was always thinking up some crazy new experiment to try out); Will Rogers (he was this actor guy who could use a lasso so well that he was actually listed in the *Guinness World Records* book for throwing three ropes at once); and Julia Childs (Ed was right—her sautéed pork chops were amazing). Sometimes Mel came over and we let her choose. Once she challenged us to a race against Olympic runner Jesse Owens. We lost. By a lot.

Every few months, if he was in town, we'd catch up with Frank DiCarlo/Al Capone and grab an ice cream with him or something. He was a really cool guy, despite his, you know, shady reputation and questionable sense of style. Ed was right; he was the best guy to protect *Pandora's Other Book*. He was killer-good with a machine gun, and he loved life too much to want to be stuck in that book again.

And of course, every Tuesday and Thursday, I hung out with Ed. The first day I went back, I couldn't wait to check out the grandfather clock. Something told me that the message Ed had left there had to do with me. And from Mel's strange reaction, I was determined to find out what it was.

But Ed had other ideas.

"Touch that clock, Spencer old boy, and I'll have Miss Margaret in here so fast, your head will spin," he said, when I made a beeline for it that first Tuesday.

I whipped around and faced him.

"Come on, Ed!" I protested. "Mel read what it said. Why can't I see it?"

I noticed the clock was working again, its pendulum swinging calmly back and forth, providing a steady rhythmic background.

He grinned. "Missed your chance, boy."

I shoved my glasses up my nose angrily. I glanced back at the clock. I'd read it someday. The old man couldn't live forever, right? Until then, I'd wait. And wonder.

Some days Gregor joined me at Ed's. Sometimes even Mel came. We'd play around with *Pandora's Book* or Ed would get us all going in a game of poker. But most days, he and I would head out to the railroad tracks to watch the 4:21 train come by and talk about what I ate for lunch. He might tell me stories about the war—some of which I was pretty sure were made up, but I didn't care. Ed's a good storyteller.

Which is a skill I kind of hope he's passed on to me. He's always telling me, "Details, kid. Life is in the details." I've tried to include as many as possible so you'd know what it was like when we had our adventure with the Evil German Guy (which is the way I'll always think of him).

Ed has warned me that there are others out there like him; people who want to use these books for bad purposes. That I have to be on guard constantly and that the day will come when I'll have to defend it again.

And when that day comes, the way things are

going with my vision, I may not even be able to see at all.

But I'll have Gregor. And Mel, I hope. And maybe Socrates and Roosevelt. And Frank DiCarlo. And I'll have *Pandora's Book*. So I'll be good.

ERIN FRY is also the author of *Losing It* and *The Benefactor*. She lives in Glendora, California, with her family. Learn more: **www.erinmfry.com**.